JUDE

THE FALLEN

<u>Jude; The Fallen</u>

Tara S. Wood and Lorecia Goings

Published by Moon Rose Publishing.

Copyright © Tara S. Wood and Lorecia Goings 2014

The right of Tara S. Wood and Lorecia Goings to be identified as the authors of this work has been asserted in accordance with sections 77 and 78 of the Copyright, Designs and Patents Act 1988

ISBN-13: 978-1-909816-39-8

The Fallen Series

Lucius; The Fallen (Book 1)

Jude; The Fallen (Book 2)

Elijah; The Fallen (Book 3, coming soon!)

Acknowledgments

First, and always, to the most supportive husband in the universe....I love you.

To my fabulous family at Moon Rose Publishing: your love and enthusiasm for this project never fails to make me feel all warm and fuzzy inside. I'm so blessed to be a part of your organization.

Last, and never least, to Sabrina Dahlgren: Madame, I am so grateful for your friendship. I don't think anyone loves these boys as much as you. Thank you so much for all of your kind words and gentle prodding to get it finished. – Tara S. Wood

Dedication

To Lori; from Tara and everyone at Moon Rose Publishing, we love and appreciate you so much, and your talent shines through this book.

JUDE
THE FALLEN

"Remember, angel, all ways in the end return to Me."

CHAPTER ONE

Lucifer stood naked at the edge of the balcony, hands wrapped around the wrought-iron railing while his snow-white wings unfurled into the cold Alpine night. Eyes bright with the quicksilver of starlight sparkled as the frigid breeze blew in from the north, pricking his pale skin with the sharp twinge of each fierce gust. He didn't care. He loved the cold. Loved the feeling of the chilled air filtering through his feathers, tangling between each one like the touch of a lover's hand. So much better than the fires of eternal damnation. For the past three months, anyway.

Lesser beings would have called his escape to Earth cowardice. And they would have been flayed alive for it. He chose to call it self-preservation. A personality trait which had served him well for thousands of years. He smirked, thinking of all he had left behind, and everything he had gained in the wake of free will. Where his brethren had chosen to fall, he had chosen to soar.

His time of self-imposed isolation here in the wonderfully icy splendor of the Swiss Alps would come to an end at some point, of that he was certain. The Liar had failed in her capture of The Catalyst, having met her end by the hand of a fallen angel. Scuttlebutt was that The Almighty himself had intervened, restoring the angel Lucius to his former glory. While the tale had all the panache of a flashy Hollywood screenplay, the knowledge tasted like ash in his mouth.

Lucius. An angel he once followed. An angel he once broke. That was comforting, at least.

And as much as he enjoyed the pain and suffering of others, the punishment of The Liar at her failure was not something he wanted to witness. Or experience. The wrath of the Dark Lord was all-consuming, leaving retreat to burn brightly as the best option at the time.

So he had scuttled away, sneaking off to regroup and plan the best way to stay in his Lord's good graces. And possibly indulge himself in carnal pleasures while he lamented his return. Lucifer's lips curved into a smile. He turned away from the frosty winds, back to the warmth of the bedroom.

The young woman on the lushly appointed bed was still, eyes open and glassy in eternal sleep. Humans broke so easily. A design flaw which, after a while, became annoying. She was the fourth this month alone. The fleshed simply couldn't stand up to his...ministrations. They weakened far too quickly, and were possessed of brittle bones he had neither the time nor the inclination to heal. It was tedious.

He wanted more. No, he needed more. Required it as he needed air to fill his lungs. Something, someone not of this world. A vision of dark hair and almond-shaped eyes came to him. A goddess. *His* goddess. He could all but smell the exotic scent of her, taste the sweet spice of her lips. Yes, Khemhry was for him and him alone. His goddess would be able to take the pleasure...and the pain.

His groin tightened painfully as he grew hard with want. Maybe it was time to leave Switzerland, after all. A visit to his goddess might be just the thing he needed to clear his head and regain focus. His cock swelled. Yes, just the thing.

With a sharp pain, his bones began to ache, and a thunderous rumbling sounded in his ears. His eyes went wide with panic as the pain came, arcing through him, pulling and clawing without mercy.

Lucifer dropped to his knees in agony as he felt himself split apart, shifting planes.

"No!" he screamed over and over again, fingers curling into the floor with futility. A second later he was gone from the room.

His respite was at an end.

Coriander drew in a short breath and held it tight. She leaned toward the cobweb-encrusted wall, brush poised to carefully dust away the detritus in her way. The painted Sanskrit was brightly colored behind the dust, and she *knew* this was the find she'd been longing for all her life. This was *the* temple. This was the place her father had been chasing, and she had done the same for over twenty-five years now. This was the temple of the Sumerian gods. It had started about a year ago, when she found a tablet and her lucky artifact. The tablet had been hard to decipher, and now rested comfortably behind glass in her office, while the charm hung from her neck by a delicate gold chain. Coriander Daphne Rhodes was used to finding things. She always found things. Whether it was the way out of a tomb or the way into the sunken chambers of Atlantis, Cori always knew the way.

A civilization's mythology always fascinated her. So when she found a grave far older than the entirety of Achilles's Tomb within the bowels of the tomb, she'd started digging. That was how she found the tablet, on a pile of bone dust, along with her artifact. The artifact, she was pretty sure, was the key to everything *big*.

Echoes of sound bounced down to her and Coriander flinched. Once again, she leaned back, turning her head to take a breath. Sounds meant someone would find her eventually and screw up everything. The temple had been gorgeous, completely virgin territory. Coriander had thrown credentials and money as fast as possible at the Turkish government so they'd give her permission to go into the temple. It was her baby.

The vibration from her pocket caught her attention and she pulled out her phone, glancing at the screen. Persephone. It wasn't the first time her sister had tried to contact her over these last few months, and she still couldn't bring herself to answer. She let the call go to voicemail, and rolled her eyes as the counter lit up. Twenty-five text messages and fifteen voicemails. Coriander had to give it to her sister; she was nothing if not persistent.

If she was being honest, she would admit that she missed Persephone. But honesty was not her best quality. And there was the small (infinitesimal, really), tiny grudge she was clinging to in the wake of Persephone's foolish devotion to Veronica. Coriander's lip curled. *Whore.* She wondered what happened to the devious blonde woman in her absence. Hopefully something painful. Possibly a raging STD.

It had been too much to bear; Persephone's effortless betrayal of their sisterly bond, coupled with the confusing and infuriating introduction of one tall, brooding fallen angel into her life. If the fallout with Persephone wasn't bad enough, there was Jude. *Bastard.*

In hindsight, she did what she did best. Moved on. She had hoped it would be an out-of-sight, out-of-mind situation, but as the months went on, her thoughts inevitably circled back to the way she left her sister. And the way she left Jude. Coriander blew out a harsh breath as Jude's face swam into her vision. It had only taken days for his presence to cement itself firmly in her path. An irritating accomplishment at best. She didn't want to think too long or too hard on what that quick connection meant. Thoughts like that only led to sleepless nights and small bouts of tears.

Leaving was imperative. She had work to do, and a course of destiny from which she could not be deterred. Her sister's lover, Lucius, and his band of feather-heads were in her way. And when confronted with the knowledge that the big angel was going to be a brick wall between her and her mission, she altered her trajectory. If she couldn't move him, she would move around him. She had moved around the globe in fact, finally coming to light here, in a deep, underground temple in Istanbul. It was almost like coming home.

She breathed again, held it and turned. Her eyes narrowed as she saw a drop of water. Without hesitation, Coriander's brush touched the wall, and she sucked in a hard breath. The dust and cobwebs drifted to the floor. A flash of red glared at her. The Sanskrit looked almost angry as it declared, *"This is home dedicated to the Most Merciful Death, Wife of the Glorious Ba'al and the Most Honored King of Fertility and the Field, Hamma-"*

Coriander shrieked as the remainder crumbled. She sank to a crumbled piece of a pillar, hands to face, and cried softly. Detritus fell from above in a sudden shower, prompting her to reach for her gun and scramble to move out of the way. She sighed as Alex's dark, curling head popped in, eyes wide.

"Whoa. Easy, Captain. I'm not worth shooting. Did you just scream?" he asked as he squeezed in.

She put her gun back in the holster, "Yeah. It fell apart again, Alex. I- I keep getting so *close*. So damned close to the end of it all. I just know this is it."

Alex sat and ran a dust-covered hand through his hair. His lips quirked into a curious smile. "You always say that, Cori. The next one will be just as good. Now, let's go grab a beer. Achmed has some on ice, not that it will last long." He held out his hand and wiggled his fingers for a second before she grabbed hold and allowed herself to be pulled up.

Neither noticed that amidst all the crumbling dust and frayed veils, a tiny hole appeared in the wall.

The sound of trickling water drifted out as the hole widened, a shaft of dappled sunlight filtering down below.

She never showed her face as she, like the archeologist, slipped through the crack. The hole in the temple wall was just large enough for her to climb through. Her sandaled foot sank into the heavy grass on the other side. She could never forget this place, this holy, sacred place...she had been born here.

The cellphone her goddess had blessed had been a lifesaver more than once. Challa pulled her veils off her head and gave a soft shake of her hair. An intricate cap of golden chain sat perfectly on top of her head as she flipped her phone open and dialed. The phone rang long enough for Challa to finish pulling off the oppressive, stifling burka. The language that was used was more ancient than the temple's heart, where Challa stood, leaning on a sculpture of Ba'al and his wife Khemyrhia in a heated embrace.

"Are you there?" her mother, Sanjeev, asked on the other end of the line.

"Of course I am. It's still as pure as it should be. What do you want me to do?" Challa bit her lip at her impertinence and waited, her foot tapping a staccato.

Her mother sighed a gentle, yet irritated sigh. "Mistress says to raze the temple. Bring it....bring it down, Challa."

"But, Mother! It will –"

"I know, Challa. Just destroy the building! Do as your mother says," Sanjeev snapped. "Go ahead. Destroy the Mistress's power. Per her command. *We must follow.*" The line went dead and Challa cursed. She bit back a sob as she pulled out a wad of C4, a detonator, and a small timer. She looked up at the sculpture and stroked Ba'al's well-muscled arm, remembering. Amidst the clearing, another sculpture hid between several trees, his eyes closed with an expression of heartache on his face.

Challa gently placed the explosives between the lovers, then pulled it back, deciding to defy her goddess. As she turned to go, a voice, rich and smoky, drifted into the clearing.

"BRING IT DOWN, CHALLA. YOU SHALL INVOKE MY WRATH, AND I SHALL COLLECT UPON YOUR MOTHER'S DEBT, SHOULD YOU DEFY ME. DO. IT. NOW."

Challa shuddered and quickly stuck the package on the statues, setting the timer. With tears in her eyes, she slipped back out to join the other workers. She knew better than to defy the goddess.

It had once been known as the Lover's Pool. But that was thousands of years past. In the moonlight that shone down upon the glen, the statues of Khemrhyia and Ba'al looked almost alive, their stony flesh entwining over a pool. A hand, so graceful and black-clawed, picked up the explosives package with a sigh. With his sigh, the grasses erupted in flowering growth and the pool overflowed. He could barely remember this place, but he remembered the Goddess Khemrhyia, and felt love. He hissed in pain as the emotion burned through his chest.

"I'nanna…," he whispered as memories of the time before came back to him. This was love, and he hungered for it. The Incubus groaned, a subtle shiver of pleasure rolling through him. He was starving. Vines twisted and writhed against his shins. He used to savor that feeling, until the fire…until he became and was born. The vines brushed his crotch, and the Incubus whimpered, rolling his hips in sexual need. It was time to feed. He looked up at the moonlight one last time and whispered, "I'nanna…where are you?"

The Incubus moaned and rolled his hips, the vines twining tight on his thighs. He gripped the small bundle of explosives as he shuddered. It was simple to switch the timer off and deactivate the detonator. He tossed the C-4 in the pool and pulled away from the vines as his eyes faded to fuchsia from black.

It was time to feed.

Finding prey was always simple. Throughout time, he'd moved through the world, each moment, each individual lover a trophy he savored. As he slipped from the temple, the Incubus inhaled the air around the campground. Scents of men and women greeted him. He paused in minor consideration. Lamplight flickered from a nearby tent, and the smell and outline of a woman, well in season and fertile, blew to him. He smiled. This was too perfect. All he had to do was wait until she was asleep. He waited.

Challa had been doing this for years. She'd always been on sites for the Sumerian gods. It was her obligation to keep them safe, keep them hidden away from the prying eyes of those who did not serve them. As a girl, she'd learned all about the cruel God-King En'lil and his gracious sister of all things bountiful, I'nanna. She always loved the tales of the Lord of Beasts, Enkidu and drew comfort from the Fertile One, Hammad. She had always served Khemrhyia, her Merciful Death. The camp was asleep, and it was only a couple of hours before her bomb would go off in the garden. She shuffled to the tent she shared with Yasmine. As she reached for the tent flap, Yasmine let out a throaty moan and Challa did not hesitate. The tent was dark, yet a soft light shone from Yasmine's bed.

She was fucking someone. His lean frame was hunched over her, rocking in a rhythm that she knew from Apollo's visits to her mistress. Her friend's squeals of pleasure made heat rise in her cheeks. The man's dark head swiveled in her direction.

It was his eyes, so frighteningly familiar, that made Challa's breath catch: They burned a fiery pink, almost the color of blood. A demon. Her mother had always warned against encounters with them. Carefully, she began to draw power to her. He hissed and his eyes widened. He blinked, and instantly his eyes were a soft brown as he whispered a questioning, "Sanjeev?"

His eyes, so full of sadness, were the deep, loamy color of turned soil. Challa blinked and he was gone. Memories, faded like the Sanskrit that wasn't carved into stone, flooded her mind: A man smiling down at her, holding her close in the warmth of his sun-kissed arms as he kissed her mother in love. Challa shook her head. No memories ever had the effect of making her weep as she curled onto her cot, missing home and her mother.

Lucius smiled into the darkness of the alley. The air was thick with the smell of blood, and heavy with the sound of labored breathing. It took him a second to register the origin of the noise. It was Domniel, breathing heavily from the rear.

"Dom? You alright back there, brother? You sound winded."

The response was a snort and a garbled grunt.

"I got my eyes on him, he's fine. Twitchy, but fine," came Jude's reply. "I think he's in the zone."

Lucius paused and turned to face his brothers. "Alright. Like always. And no hero shit. I'm not spending another night feeling one of you up to make sure your bones knit properly." He frowned. "I'm looking at you, Cai."

Mordecai grinned. "If it helps, you made the ugliest night nurse ever."

"I mean it," Lucius said. The deaf angel gave him a thumbs up. "Fine. Let's see what's waiting for us."

He was two steps in when the ambush came from behind, from the open air of the deserted street. Domniel shouted, and he heard the sound of gunfire before he could wheel around to get perspective. Bright flashes blinked against the dark of night as Domniel popped off two more rounds into the pack of demons that rushed them.

Lucius lost sight of the others as he connected with a demon, the force of the tackle shoving him into the alley. He landed on his back with a grunt, dropping his .45, and his head hit the concrete with enough force to make his teeth rattle. Something warm and wet seeped through the fabric of his shirt. Blood.

The demon hissed above him, baring jagged yellow teeth, its breath reeking of brimstone. His hands came up to catch the demon at its sides, and he grabbed hold, yanking backwards over his head to send it flying into a dumpster with a metallic clang. Lucius scrambled to his feet and back out to the fray, snatching up his piece. His brothers needed him.

Mordecai and Elijah stood back to back, anchoring each other as they grappled with a demon each. Neither angel had the upper hand, and Lucius' eyes flicked between them as he raised his weapon.

"Lige! Hit the deck!" he shouted.

The silent angel's head jerked to look at his leader, narrowly missing a bite to the face. His grip on the demon in front of him faltered and he reached back with both hands to grab onto Mordecai. Elijah's left leg curled back to hook around Mordecai's right. He yanked with a hard, downward pull at the same time he swept Mordecai's leg, and both angels crumpled to the concrete, leaving the two demons wide open. The muzzle on his .45 flashed twice in succession, and both headshots were true, sending blood and brain matter spraying out into the air.

"You alright?" Lucius called in Elijah's direction. Elijah grabbed Mordecai's hand and raised them together in solidarity. They were fine. His eyes searched for Jude and Domniel, missing the hissing sound coming from the rear.

"Boss!" Jude called, putting three slugs in a downed demon. The big angel perked up and ran, but Domniel cut past him like he was out for a Sunday stroll, pushing Lucius to the ground and vaulting over him to catch the newly-appeared demon by the throat, disappearing into the inky blackness of the alley.

Lucius pushed up from the ground, moving to follow the blind angel into the fight. Jude's hand on his arm stopped him cold. Jude never initiated touch. The big angel jerked his arm back with a wince. "I wouldn't go in there. He's on another plane, boss. Look." Jude gestured to the pile of remains behind him. Pile was the operative word. The corpse had been ripped limb from limb, ragged, putrid flesh hanging from the joints. Arms and legs were in a jumble on top of the torso, lying where they had been thrown. Even in the darkness, he could see the distinct outline of Domniel's boot print in the middle of the chest. He'd stomped on the torso to hold it down while he ripped the head off with his bare hands.

"Fuck," Lucius muttered.

"Yeah," Jude huffed. "As in 'what the actual'. Like I said, don't follow. If he needs us, we'll know." Jude moved aside to check on Elijah and Mordecai.

All they heard from the darkness was a series of screams and cracking sounds, punctuated by Domniel growling, "Do. Not. Stab. Me. Demonic. Asshole."

A few more screams, then the wet, sucking sound of steel on flesh and the stench of brimstone. The solo move would not go unmentioned, but Lucius had to admit that Domniel was frustrated. He carefully watched as Domniel emerged from the shadows and flung a knife at a rat sneaking by. The rat gave a final squeak before Lucius said, "Jesus, Dom. You killed it. Now put the blades down."

The blind angel blinked, flecks of blood spraying from his eyelashes like tiny rubies. Domniel shook his head and said, "No. There's another one. Where did it go?"

"Who the fuck knows?" Jude grunted. "And speaking of fucking, get fucking laid, Dom."

Domniel tilted his head, the blank gaze unnerving without the shades, and tightened his jaw. "You first."

Jude ignored the warning signals as he continued, "It's been three months since you've gone fishing. Shit, look at you." A large hand waved in Domniel's direction. "You're a fucking mess, brother. You need to pop one off, stat. If you're low on cash, fuck, I'll spot you."

Mordecai sighed from the sidelines. "Seriously, Jude, I'm deaf and *I* wish you would shut the fuck up. Leave him alone. We've got better shit to do than to stand around while you ride around on your unicorn. Let's find the other demon and get the hell out of here." He frowned and rubbed one hand over his stomach. "I'm hungry."

Domniel sneered, a flash of white against the sticky redness of his skin. He pointed one of the blades at them, his face tired, and said, "You know what? Get fucked, Jude. So what if it's been three months since I got laid? Is that really any of your goddamned business? Butt. The. Fuck. Out."

The whisper of something falling caused Domniel to jerk, the blade leaving his hand to hit the tumbling object. It landed with a heavy thud. The scent of sulfur was muted, as if it was dried, and another smell wafted up from the body. Lucius eyed it warily. It was almost mummy-like, skin desiccated and peeled away from its face, its mouth wide open, displaying all its teeth. The demon's corpse was definitely a problem.

"Lige, Cai, go check up top for anyone else," Lucius said. "And for the love of Christ, Dom. Put the damn knife down."

CHAPTER TWO

The living room was quiet, save for the sound of breathing, and the occasional rasp of paper as Elijah and Mordecai flipped through their books. Lucius and Persephone reclined in a tangle of limbs on one sofa, relaxed in a happy state of contentment. Jude was folded into a club chair on the opposite side of the room, eyes shut as he dozed. Beneath him on the floor, Domniel lay against the front of the upholstered chair. He rested quietly, soaking in the proximity, but not quite touching the big angel's frame. In the middle of the room, underneath the coffee table, a small, black and gray bundle of fur snored with little whuffs of breath. Princess, as Persephone had introduced the badger, seemed oblivious to the addition of people into the house.

The serenity of the scene soon erupted into chaos as a growing clatter of noise drifted in from outside. The sound of engines was sharp and stuttered, overshadowed by the larger din of drumming.

Persephone perked up with a wide smile on her face as a horrified Winston tore through the room to the front door.

"No, no, no!" he shouted, his normally placid face florid with unwanted excitement. "She can't be here! Mistress Coriander said they were never to return! The lawn! The gardens! They're murder on my flowerbeds!"

The angels snorted awake as Persephone gasped and poked at her lover. "Lucius, come on! She's here!"

"Who's here?" he grumbled, getting to his feet.

The butler pulled the heavy double doors open and groaned as sunlight spilled into the living room. "Oh no," he cried, looking out at the gravel drive. "Miss Persephone, stop her! They can't-they just can't!"

Persephone laughed, and shot past Lucius as the other angels moved in step behind him to see what waited beyond the front door. Persephone's laughter was lost in the noise coming from outside, and she gripped Winston's shoulders from behind, shaking him gently.

"It's just Teir, Winston. And a few of her mates." She ran out the door and down the drive, arms wide open in invitation, calling out over the raucous sound of Celtic music. "Teraslynn! You're back!"

Four large, beat-up VW vans rolled into the drive, garishly painted with Celtic symbols in bright, mismatched colors. The doors opened, and multitudes of people spilled out onto the lawn, causing the butler to emit a high-pitched squeak of disapproval.

"What is it, Winston? Why the commotion? Who is it?" Lucius asked.

The butler stammered, but finally edged out, "Miss Teraslynn. Mistress Coriander and Miss Persephone's sister." He huffed, straightening his waistcoat before stomping off. "I've got to stop them! They'll ruin the grass!"

Figures danced their way across the drive, avoiding the harried butler and his waving arms, spreading out to the front yard to lay blankets and bags on the grass. They moved with a frenetic grace, laughing, chattering, and singing, while others unpacked the vans. One figure from the first van emerged, tall and regal, even with green streaks through her blond hair, her expression lighting up as she caught sight of Persephone running toward her.

The two women caught each other up in a fierce hug, taking turns spinning each other around and laughing like children. Teraslynn was a good head taller than her petite counterpart, long and lean in a blousy, thin shirt that hung off of one milky shoulder. Her legs were graceful and coltish, wrapped in soft green leggings with leather boots that laced up to the knee. Strands of bells were attached to the laces, jingling noisily as she and Persephone reunited.

It was loud and chaotic, and the angels stood in the doorway, mouths agape like the butler, while Domniel clapped his hands over his ears.

"What's all this racket? I was napping, for fuck's sake," the blind angel complained.

"Another sister?" Jude exclaimed. "Christ, how many are there?"

Lucius shook his head as he stared at Persephone's smiling face. "I don't know, bro. But I don't think he's the one you need to ask."

Winston's hand trembled as he pulled his cell phone from his pocket. He was *very* unhappy. They all thought he wouldn't do it, that he could not get his mistress to come home to deal with all these...mongrels. He cradled a bright red peony in his other hand as he flipped his phone open and pressed the power button. His peonies. *The animals.* He closed his eyes and blew out a breath. She had to come home. She had to.

Coriander's head lifted, her eyes instantly covered in soap suds as she patted around the counter top for her phone, which warbled out a tinny version of Nickelback's

"Hero". Finally, after several moments, she realized her boob was vibrating and shoved a wet hand into her cleavage.

"What, Winston?"

The sounds of sniffling were the only thing on the other end of the phone before Winston said, "They did it, madam. You should come home immediately."

"I'm on a dig, Winston. What the hell are you talking about?"

"I'm talking about *them*. They're here. They have positively destroyed, no, annihilated my gardens! My grass, my lawn, the fountains, the roses, my *award-winning peonies*! All of it! Destroyed!"

She waited for his hysterics to pass. "Your peonies? Really? Exactly what are you talking about?"

"That herd of Irish mongrels that your foul-mouthed cow of a drunken sister has deposited here!" he shrieked.

Coriander frowned. "Teir's there?" He could mean no other by the bovine reference, since the time she got drunk and ate all the bread in Coriander's house. Winston still shuddered at her chewing. She could already hear her sister's bells as she said, "Fine. Alex and I will stop for Ash and then we'll be home. You can handle them until then. You've done it before. Just think of Keith Richards on a binge and you'll be fine."

His tone was imperious. "Absolutely not! I will quit before I deal with the garden-destroying wild pigs and your booze-swilling angelic lot-"

"Wait." Coriander's frown deepened into a scowl. Her sisters always had an open invitation, but there shouldn't be anyone else at her place. "Who is in residence, Winston?" As she listened to Winston sob his way through the listing of everyone at her house,

Coriander's eyes narrowed, her hand shook as it clenched the phone, and her lips tightened into a fine line. Persephone was dead, and so was Teraslynn for hurting her favorite butler's peonies.

She slammed the wet phone onto the bathroom counter and yelled out into the bedroom, "Alex! Call your mother! We're getting Ash and going home! And I'm murdering two of my sisters!"

Just when he thought it couldn't get any louder, the front door opened and Coriander walked through. Jude watched as the heated argument in the living room between Persephone, Teraslynn, and Winston shifted from shouting about peonies, common decency, and tolerance, to an ear-splitting cacophony of squealing, laughing, and giggling. The butler immediately broke from the chaos and scuttled to the front door, taking Coriander's bags as her sisters scooped her into a giant three-way hug.

Two more figures emerged in the doorway, a tall, tanned, dark-haired man, and a small girl clutching a sparkly, green stuffed dragon. His stomach hit the floor as he stared at the child. She couldn't have been more than four or five, but it was the combination of features that stopped him cold. Her long, red hair curled into a familiar fashion, and her green eyes looked back at him with a cool appraisal he had seen before. She was fine boned and lithe, her frame so similar to the good-looking man standing beside her. This was Coriander's child. And the dark-haired stranger looking way too at ease in her foyer had to be the father. *Fuck.*

The squealing continued for a minute before Coriander extricated herself and glared at her sisters.

"This is not a Holiday Inn, ladies! Now what the hell are you all doing here?"

The dark-haired man cleared his throat and raised an eyebrow at Coriander before glancing down at the girl.

"Right. Ash is here. Watch your mouths," Coriander said. Reaching back for the girl, she continued, "Ashtiru, sweetie, be polite. Say hello to your Aunt Sephie and Aunt Teir."

The little girl's lips parted in a wide smile so much like Coriander's, Jude's breath caught in his throat. She rushed from her father's side, and her aunts scooped her up for another round of hugging.

Coriander turned to face him, and her glance cut past him to Lucius, Mordecai, and Elijah. She frowned. "Where's Dominick?"

"It's Domniel," Lucius said. "He's in the pool house. He doesn't come down much."

She didn't reply, but turned to the man at the door. "Are you coming in or what? I told you I don't care if you stay, but Ash would probably like you to be here for a few days."

"Then I'll stay." His Greek accent was sharp and thick, but the words were soft. "Besides," he glanced at the angels, "you haven't introduced me to your friends."

Jude couldn't hold back the snort and the other man's eyebrow lifted again.

Coriander sighed. "Sure. Alex Kiriakis, this is Lucius, Mordecai, Elijah, and Jude. Guys, this is Alex, my business partner. And that," she pointed to the little girl, who was now tucked in on the sofa between her aunts, quickly becoming the victim of a vicious tickle, "is our daughter, Ashtiru."

Paternity confirmed. Double fuck.

"Persephone didn't mention you had a child," Lucius offered.

"Well, she sure didn't tell me that you had invaded my home, so I guess she's keeping secrets from all of us," Coriander shot back.

Persephone's voice was light as she continued tickling Ashtiru, "If you checked your messages ever, you would have known, Cori."

Coriander glanced her way and frowned. "Point taken. So, would someone fill me in on why my butler has lost his grip on sanity? This sort of ruckus is just the kind of thing that will send him to an early grave."

"Winnie's too high-strung by far, Cori," Teraslynn replied in her Irish lilt. "We offered him a good swig o' Jameson's and a seat in the drumming circle, but the ol' bastard cursed at me and went on." She giggled and covered Ashtiru's ears with her hands. "Sorry." She giggled louder and shouted out into the room after the absent butler, "Ye uptight fecker!" She shook her head and hugged Ashtiru to her chest. "Too attached to his florals, he is."

"I'm attached to those peonies, Teir! Do you know how much it cost me to have the freaking things jetted in from France? Ugh!" She threw her hands up and pointed at Ashtiru. "You. Bed. It's way past your bedtime." Coriander turned to Alex. "Take her up, will you? I'll be there to tuck her in soon."

He nodded. "Evening, all." Alex held out his arms. "Come on, princess. Time for bed."

Ashtiru snatched up her stuffed dragon from the floor and ran into her father's waiting arms. Her little red head buried itself in the crook of Alex's neck as he walked to the stairs. Princess eagerly followed behind. As he passed by, Jude felt a ripple in the air, and the scent of sand and spice filtered into his nostrils. It was familiar and strange all at once, and he looked harder at the side of Alex's face as he ascended the stairs. Hovering around him was a light blue glow that flickered in soft pulses. At the apex, over Alex's mess of dark curls, the image coalesced. He glanced over at Lucius, to confirm that he wasn't losing his mind. Sure enough, his leader had his gaze firmly attached to the other man. No, Lucius saw it too. Alex disappeared onto the second floor and Jude whipped around to Lucius.

He leaned over and whispered, "You see that, boss?"

Lucius nodded, his face grim. "Yeah. I saw it. You think Cori knows?"

Jude shrugged. There was no telling what sort of things the archeologist knew. Nothing seemed to faze her, and the image of an ancient dog filtering around her boyfriend wasn't exactly the sort of thing to come up in casual conversation. "Want me to ask her?"

"Yeah," Lucius replied, "but give it a day or two. I think she's a bit shell-shocked from finding us here."

"Not to mention the fuck-all racket that is Teraslynn and her Ren Faire Rejects," Jude added.

Elijah's hands flickered from the other end of the living room. "I think the Irish one is refreshing."

Jude smiled at him and gave him his middle finger.

The child's bedroom was decorated all in pink. It was a confection of bright, fluffy love, tiaras, and Dora the Explorer, that sort of exploded. Ashtiru loved it. Her bed, a four-post version of Coriander's, but with a higher lip, had her favorite quilt; a blanket with a pastel green and blue dragon embroidered upon it. Coriander watched as she flounced on it, fluffing out her quilt. Princess waddled to the edge and rose on her two back feet. Alex picked her up while Coriander proceeded to change Ashtiru into her Hello Kitty pajamas.

The girl yawned as Coriander picked up the story book and asked, "Mommy? Are we going to be staying here a while?"

"For a little bit," she answered as searched for her last place in the book, "Why do you ask?"

"I don't want to go away from you and Daddy," Ashtiru answered. She punched her pillow to make Princess a nest to snuggle next to her head. Alex sat on the other side, checking his cell phone's messages and texts.

"Well, you're not going anywhere that Mommy and Daddy will never find you. Now, let's catch up with Mr. Badger and Mr. Toad, shall we?" Coriander said as she perched her glasses upon her nose and started reading.

It only took five minutes of reading until Ashtiru's eyes drifted closed, arms wound tight around the badger. Coriander thanked the gods for jet lag. On silent feet, both parents kissed their little girl goodnight and crept from the room. Coriander stopped in the hallway to put away her glasses, and felt the heat of Alex's body press solid against hers. He sighed and leaned in to brush his lips against her neck. Coriander stepped away, barely able to contain her irritation as she spun on her heel to glare at him, "What the hell are you doing?" she hissed through clenched teeth.

"Obviously nothing tonight," he snarked. He leaned against the wall and crossed his arms while pouting, "I was hoping that we could get closer, but I'm guessing you don't want that."

Coriander's mouth hardened. "You know the answer to that. What prompted this?" He opened his mouth, but the brief pause told her she wouldn't be able to trust his words. Her eyes narrowed as she said, "You've got some fucking nerve, Alex. I am not your damn fire hydrant. You will not piss on me and then trot off to someone else. Quit being a jealous man." She stamped her foot and whirled to go to her bedroom. "Asshole."

Alex sighed and rubbed his temples. It was time to drink.

Jude stared at the blinding white of the bathroom tiles, gleaming back at him with their pristine cleanliness. There was a reason he was here, a reason he stood at the threshold of the doorway with the small blade in his hand. It was a steely and dangerous little thing he'd nicked from Elijah as soon as they got here. He missed the obsidian dagger. He hadn't realized how much. The Almighty had seen fit to take it and transform it into a demon-killing sword that belonged in the hands of Lucius. Now it was gone. Much like its previous owner, lost to him in every way. Coriander belonged to the dark-haired Alex and the little girl. He didn't belong to anyone.

The tremor started in his foot and worked its way up his leg, urging him to take the step into the bathroom, but he could not make it move. His vision warped and tunneled outward, and the bathroom rippled, beckoning him to breach the door jamb. Seeing her walk through the door had ripped open every wound he thought had healed. And even though she had made it perfectly clear she wanted nothing to do with him when she left, there was the tiny, hidden part of him that held on to the memory of his lips on hers. Because there had been no pain.

Everything hurt. All the time. Touch was agony. But when his lips met hers, the expected jolt never came. She had been hot and sweet, and the release from the pain had been instant, snuffed out like a candle. And when she shot him, it all came back. If he were honest with himself, he could admit to being grateful for the slug to the leg. He was so used to the constant and ever-present ache in his body and bones, and the sudden reprieve at Coriander's kiss had thrown him for a loop. The gunshot simply grounded him.

Now she was back in his life, all guns and fire and fierce beauty, with a boyfriend and kid in tow. And here he was, back in this never-ending ritual of pleasure-pain that kept him in a perpetual vacillation between guilt and despair.

No. He was done with this. Never again.

Jude dropped the blade to clatter on the tile floor of the bathroom and turned on his heel. There were other ways to deal with this problem. It was time to drink.

CHAPTER THREE

Jude stumbled down the hallway through the living room, clutching the empty bottle of Wild Turkey to his chest. Through the alcoholic haze, he could make out a sliver of light coming from underneath a closed door just off the living area. Ah, the parlor. He'd seen the fractious butler sneak a nip of brandy in that room once or twice. Got to be more where that came from.

He opened the door with more force than he intended, and it swung back to hit the door stop with a loud thud. The sound of a safety clicking sobered him for a second and he dove to the floor, reaching for a non-existent Glock. *Fuck.*

"Who's there?" a slurred Greek voice demanded. Great. The boyfriend. *Double fuck.*

"It's Jude. Put your damn piece away before you shoot me," he called from the floor. He looked up to see Alex's rumpled head peeking down at him from over the chaise.

"Oh, yeah. Sorry. Force of habit," Alex said. "Gun's down. You can get up now."

Jude eased to his feet, closing his eyes against the nausea that rolled up at his sudden ascent to upright. "Jesus, you should be more careful with that thing. You could have shot me."

"Kind of the point."

Jude snorted, and came around to set the empty bottle on the table in the middle of the room. He noticed his bottle wasn't alone. His gaze flicked to Alex. The dark-haired man was glassy-eyed and disheveled, and he swayed a little on the chaise. "New bottle, then?" he asked.

Alex grunted in approval. "Behind you. In the lower cabinet."

Jude turned and walked over to the cabinet, opening the bottom door. "Do you have a preference?" *Like I give a fuck.*

"Strong."

Jude grabbed a bottle of Grey Goose and two glasses from the counter. He returned to sit in the large club chair and poured two hefty glasses of the booze. He held one out to Alex.

Alex reached out with a long-fingered hand and accepted. Before Jude could let go, Alex eyed him over the glass. "If you think I don't know what's going on, you're an idiot," he said.

Jude returned the glare. "If you think you know what's going on, then you're the idiot." He let go of the glass and sat back to stare at Alex as he sipped the vodka. The blue glow was back, flickering with enough effect to hurt Jude's eyes. He knew he should be able to place both the light and the image that hovered over him, but the knowledge seemed even more removed from his brain under the fog of alcohol. Something was off, and not being able to put his finger on it was irritating.

"I know more than you think I do, angel." Alex's voice was hard.

"Who are you?" The words slipped out in a vodka-scented rush before he could stop them.

Alex laughed, then hiccupped. "Not of this world. Same as you. But different."

Jude frowned. "That doesn't make any sense."

"Does everything need to make sense in your world? Or don't you have any faith?"

His jaw clenched and his hand tightened around the crystal glass. "I don't think that's any of your business."

"Maybe," Alex countered, leaning forward with a sly smile. "But Cori is my business. In more ways than one." Alex's eyes narrowed and he snorted. "I don't like you."

Jude smiled. "And here I was worried my dislike wouldn't be reciprocated. That's a weight off my shoulders."

"I would hate to disappoint."

Jude slammed the glass back, sucking down the rest of the vodka. The burn was instant, and he hissed against it. The bastard smiled at him across the table.

"For some reason she likes you," Alex admitted. "I have no fucking clue why, from everything she's told me, but she does."

Jude poured another glass. "How do you figure?"

"She shot you, right?"

He grunted.

"And you lived. Ergo, Cori likes you. She has trouble expressing herself in conventional ways."

Jude's eyebrow went up.

Alex leaned back and propped an ankle on his knee. "She talked a lot about you. It was irritating."

"Funny, she never mentioned you." The barb hit home and Alex's eyes narrowed.

"Now I really don't like you."

"Likewise." Jude looked down at his glass. Empty again. How did that happen? He reached for the bottle when Alex's empty glass appeared in his blurred field of vision. *Meh, what the hell?* He refilled both glasses.

The dark-haired Greek took a long drink from his glass and sat back with a satisfied *ah*. "She's an awful lot of woman to be so little, you know. I've seen her make Arab princes run for the dunes. She can be quite terrifying."

"Is this a sales pitch? Because if it is, it sucks."

Alex chuckled. "No, just a warning."

It was meant to sound innocent, but Jude's alcohol-soaked brain latched onto the word 'warning' like a lifeline. Before he knew it, the crystal glass dropped from his hand to roll onto the rug, and he had Alex by the throat, shoving him down into the cushioned chaise.

His hand was burning, and he could feel the fires of pain licking up his skin, burrowing down to the muscle underneath. Jude's lip curled and he spat, "Don't you fucking threaten me."

Alex's eyes were wide with shock, but Jude couldn't see fear. The blue glow around him swirled and the image over his head coalesced. Recognition set in. A jackal. The glow softened, and Jude's hand tightened as the blue light shivered to wrap around his hand.

The light was cold and icy, dampening the fires that burned on his skin. There was no relief, just a switch from burning hot to freezing cold. Jude's attention wavered, and the muzzle of Alex's gun pressed into his torso.

"Get the fuck off me," he wheezed from beneath Jude's grip.

"Not before you tell me what you are, Alex."

Alex's answer was to twist and buck at the same time, unbalancing Jude, and Alex threw him off onto the floor.

"We're done here," Alex growled, turning to stomp to the door, the nine hanging from his hand.

"Like hell," Jude snarled, scrambling to lunge forward and tackle Alex behind the knees.

Alex cried out as he fell, and the reflexive shot that popped off echoed through the air, shattering a window on the far wall. Jude snatched the gun from his hand and tossed it aside, grabbing hold of Alex's hips to flip him over. Fists flew and mouths swore as they grappled, rolling over and over until the sound of Coriander's voice filled the room.

"What the fuck is going on in here?"

Both men stilled and looked up at the pissed-off redhead in the doorway. Neither man dared to speak as they pushed apart with a final volley of half-hearted slaps and heated glares.

"Get. Up."

Jude and Alex scrambled to their feet as she entered the room in a flourish of silk, her robe fluttering behind her. She spotted the gun on the floor and snatched it up, stalking to Alex with a face like death. She shoved the piece into his hands and slapped him hard across the face. Alex's face snapped back with a start.

"You fucking idiot! What were you thinking? Your child is upstairs! *Your child, Alex!*" she hissed. Her death-glare turned on Jude. "And you. I expected better than this from you. From both of you." She pointed to the double doors that led to the outside. "March."

Alex's eyes hit the floor, and he trudged over and walked outside.

"You too, pigeon," she snarled.

Jude followed him to the little cobbled courtyard and out into the grass.

He was about to turn around and demand what the hell she was doing when he was hit with a forceful spray of icy cold water. The ungainly shriek that emerged from his throat was echoed by Alex as she turned the hose on both of them. The drenching lasted for a few more seconds before she turned off the spigot and dropped the hose on the ground.

Coriander wrapped the robe around her and yanked the tie into a knot. She folded her arms over her chest and squared her shoulders. "Do not come back in this house until you sleep it off. And if this happens again, I will end the both of you." She turned and went back into the house, muttering, "Men."

Jude and Alex stared at each other with hard faces, and parted ways, the wet squishing of their feet in the grass mingling with sounds of crickets in the moonlight.

Jude awoke with a splitting headache and a mouth that tasted like cotton-stuffed shit. One eye cracked open, only to slam shut again under the painful assault of sunlight on his corneas. He groaned as the previous evening's events came back to him. Wild Turkey. Alex. Vodka. The hose.

"Are you going to get up now? It's almost lunchtime." The tiny voice filtered into his brain, cutting though the replay of bad decisions. He rolled to the side and tried opening his eyes again.

Ashtiru stood over him in a bright yellow sundress, her bare feet nestled in the grass, toes glittering with a sparkly pink polish. Her halo of red hair swirled around her oval face in the breeze, and she shifted the stuffed dragon in her grasp to swipe at a stray lock that fell over her nose.

"Are you up?" The tiny foot shot out to poke him in the side. He winced at the poke, more irritated than injured by the gesture. "Mommy said if you don't get up and come inside, then you have to stay out here." Jude watched as her nose wrinkled. "You can't stay out here. You need a bath. You smell funny."

He eased up to a sitting position, fighting against every synapse in his body that protested. Ashtiru eyed him warily, but held out a small hand. He moved as if to stand on his own, but the little girl huffed and shook her hand at him in a manner that reminded him of her mother. He wasn't afraid to touch her, but neither was he eager.

"Manners," Ashtiru blurted. "Mommy says it's polite to take someone's hand when they give it to you." She shook her hand again for emphasis. The wide-eyed innocence hit him right in the solar plexus, stealing the breath from his lungs. He gritted his teeth and grasped her hand.

There was a vibration, but no pain. It got under his skin and grated, but it was nowhere near as painful as touching anyone else. The realization was startling, and he would have spent more time dwelling on the lightbulb moment, but his stomach decided to give a violent pitch, and he turned to the side to vomit into the grass with a loud retch.

Ashtiru squealed and dropped his hand, running back to the house, shouting, "Mommy! Mommy! Mr. Jude needs the throw-up bowl!"

Coriander slammed the book shut, making her sister jump. "Have you lost your mind, Persephone? I want them out of my house. Or at least fixing the mess in the gardens."

"Cori, they need a place to stay. You've only been home three days. They've been here for three months already, and it's not like you don't have-" Persephone hated talking to her sister in the office. The whole room was designed to intimidate anyone below a genius level IQ. The ocean of dark oak spread between the overstuffed wingback chair where she sat, and across the desk where Coriander sat getting angrier by the second, made Persephone feel like she was six and in trouble all over again.

Coriander glared at her over the top of her little round reading glasses. "Room for them?" she finished. "While you may treat my house like a hotel, it is not. They're sloppy, loud, and irritating. I found Jude sitting in this very office, at *this* very desk, having phone sex, and Dominick has completely taken over my guest house."

Persephone sighed. "It's Domniel. And Lucius says that Dom needs some space to work out some issues he's having."

Coriander's face reddened and she stood up. Turning a deeper shade of red, she planted her hands on the massive desktop and bit out, "I seriously doubt that the harem of cheap whores he accumulates counts as working on his fucking issues."

Before Persephone could stop herself, she replied, "When you put it that way, I would say that's exactly what he's doing." As soon as it was out, she slapped a hand over her mouth and watched the fine tremble that began in Coriander's hands work its way up her arms. Coriander pointed toward the door and Persephone bolted.

Shutting the door behind her on her sister's piercing cry of frustration, Persephone sighed in relief, and smiled at Lucius as he walked toward her. "Well, she didn't shoot me. That's good, right?"

"What did she say? You look like you narrowly missed being shot at." Persephone gave him a wan smile and he frowned. "She can't be that angry about us being here."

"She is." Persephone slipped an arm through Lucius' and laid her head on his bicep. "But she'll get over it." They walked back towards the living room.

"Or she'll kill us all in our sleep," he muttered.

Persephone patted his arm. "It's a distinct possibility."

Jude appeared on the landing between the hallway and the living room. He inclined his head down the length of the long hall. "She in her office?"

Persephone nodded. "Yes, but I wouldn't approach her just now. She's a bit testy."

"When isn't she?" the big angel huffed.

Lucius ushered Persephone past him and continued behind her, throwing his brother a knowing look. "Good luck. Please try to come out of there with all your limbs attached. It'll just piss off Lige if he has to heal you again. You're like the worst patient ever."

"I can't make any promises. You know what she's like."

"Yeah, and I know you," Lucius called over his shoulder. "So don't fuck it up, princess."

He didn't bother to knock before he barged into Coriander's office. Her back was turned as she perused one of the wall-to-wall bookshelves.

"And to what do I owe this honor?" Her tone dripped with sarcasm. "Here to run up my phone bill with some more of your freaky sex talk?"

"A lapse in discretion. It won't happen again," Jude replied.

"You bet your feathered ass it won't." She turned to face him, the lines of her face tight, but he could see the hint of a smile at the edge of her lips. "I know you're not all touchy-feely, but if you need someone to talk dirty to you, Teir probably wouldn't mind. I'd say sleep with her, but for one, she's my sister, and two, she'd be all over you like a bad rash. I don't think you could handle her." Her lips turned up and she grinned.

"Please tell me you just didn't offer up Teraslynn." He could feel his back starting to itch under the playfulness of that smile. "Because that's creepy."

"What? It's no secret that Teir is," she put up her fingers in air quotes, "friendly. She's a free spirit. A bit of a hedonist, actually. She loves everything about life. Music, dancing, eating, drinking...sex. Lots of sex. Why do you think half those idiots are here with her? It's not the insurance plan."

Jude shifted on his feet, trying hard to remember why he came in here in the first place. The golden tattoo on his back was burning now, catapulted into wakefulness by the images his brain was producing regarding Coriander and sex. He realized he wanted to touch her again, to get the relief he knew he would find when her skin met his. A brush of the cheek, a hand sliding down her arm, her lips on his, his tongue in her mouth, her hand wrapped around his-

"What the hell is Alex?" he blurted, cutting off the slapdash porno in his brain. "He's not human, right? He glows. Tell me you know he glows."

Coriander gave him a curious frown at his switch in the conversation, but replied smoothly, "He's an Anubis."

"A what?"

"You heard me. The word is 'Anubis'." Coriander sighed. "Really, it shouldn't be too hard for you to wrap your head around, given you are," she gestured with her hand in his direction, "what you are."

Jude snorted. "And what's that?"

"Special," she replied dryly. "In more ways than one." Ignoring his frown, she continued. "Look, it's not something I'm comfortable talking about, because it puts me precariously close to the edge of bestiality," She gave an irritated shiver. "Ew. So if you're dead set on figuring him out, I suggest you go to Alex and talk to him. Horse's mouth, er….dog and all that."

"You? Not comfortable talking about something?" Jude exclaimed, mock-surprise flitting across his face. "I don't believe it."

"Very funny," she sneered.

"Anubis. The ones with dog heads? Like werewolves?"

Coriander pinched the bridge of her nose and sighed. "Werewolves? Honestly?" She frowned. "Have you been reading Seph's romance novels again?" She shook her head and raised her hand. "No, I don't want to know. He's as human as you and…well, as human as I am, at any rate. No, he's not a," her fingers shot up with air quotes again, "shifter, or anything like that. He's just different, okay? Differently Anubis."

"'Differently'—that doesn't make any sense, Coriander."

"Nothing about my life ever makes any sense. I thought you would have figured that out by now. The fact remains that he and I are still partners of sorts. Alex and I were over romantically a long time ago, and frankly the best things to come out of our associations are Ashtiru and my fat bank account. In that order." She crossed her arms over her chest and glared. "Now, if you're finished giving me the third degree over crap that has nothing to do with you, and nothing to do with the current course of Demon-Killing One-oh-one, then we're done here." She jerked her head to the door, but Jude stood his ground, meeting her frosty look with a glare of his own.

"Do I need to be concerned?"

"About what?" she snapped.

"The safety of my brothers," he replied. "You know, kind of what we do here. Keep people safe. Is he a threat?"

"A threat?" Coriander rolled her eyes and huffed with exaggerated zeal. "Please. Alex is harmless. Well, unless you lie to him, but that's beside the point." She waved her hands around for emphasis. "What *is* important is that yes, he is the father of my child, no, we're not together anymore, and whether you like it or not, he will be around. So you can either try to play nice and get along with him, or you can politely get the fuck out of my house. Understand?"

He ignored the comment. "There is another matter I want to discuss with you. The one I came in here for, actually."

She sat down at her desk and started to rifle through some paperwork. "And what's that?"

"You owe me an apology, Coriander."

She responded with an unladylike snort.

"I'm serious, Coriander."

"So am I." Was he going to keep saying her name like that? *Coriander.* He drew out all four syllables, just like her mother when she was well on her way to being pissed. That needed to stop.

She looked up from her paperwork and studied him. He was a man on a mission, his face hard with determination. She knew that look. Men trembled in fear and scrambled to get the hell out of his way when he wore that expression. It was move or fucking be moved. But there was something else lurking behind the dark sapphire of his eyes. Something softer and infinitely more terrifying.

"I mean it. You owe me an apology." The rumble in his voice sent a hot shiver down her spine.

He was so not playing fair, coming into her office looking all dangerous and sexy. Sexy? She groaned, and she frowned at him for flustering her.

"You need to unclench. Your jaw is so sharp I could shave my legs on it." She arched an eyebrow at him. "And I disagree. I have nothing to apologize for." She folded her hands primly on the wide expanse of lacquered wooden desktop.

"You shot me!" Jude exclaimed, the ferocity rearing its head. "Twice!" he added.

Coriander pointed a stabby finger at him and furrowed her brows in indignation. "You *kissed* me!"

"Once!" he yelled, redness coloring his cheeks. "I kissed you once!"

"Yeah, well it deserved two slugs!" she shot back, popping up from the chair.

"Coriander!" he growled.

"Don't you 'Coriander' me!" she snapped. "You're not my mother! And this is my house! *My* house! You and the rest of the flock can't just barge in here while I'm out of town and start telling me what to do! I mean, you just came in and took over!" she cried. A fiery red curl popped free from her ponytail as her head shook in frustration.

Her finger jabbed in the air more viciously this time as she continued the tirade, "Poor Winston-"

"What about him? Nobody's touched the butler!" Jude argued.

"What about him?" She was near to screaming now. "He's *English*, for chrissakes! The raciest thing to come through this house while I'm gone is Ovaltine! Cleaning up after Domniel alone has almost given him apoplexy! Twice!" she sputtered. "If he hadn't buttled for The Stones in the late sixties, you boozy pigeons would have sent him over the edge!" She threw her hands up and groaned loudly. "My sister Teraslynn and the pack of screeching micks she hangs with aren't even this bad! But put you all together, and suddenly my place is a goddamned commune!"

Jude crossed his arms and frowned at her, the hard mask back in place. "You're changing the subject. I came for an apology. I will get one."

The set in his stance and the steel of his spine irritated her beyond words. She picked up the crystal paperweight from the desk and chunked it at him full force, the exasperated scream echoing off the office walls. He sidestepped with a duck and it hit the bookcase next to him, shattering as it crashed to the floor.

"Get out. Get out now." Her voice was like stone.

He opened his mouth to reply, but shadows crossed his eyes, and he turned on silent feet to leave the room.

The air whooshed from her lungs in one long breath as she sat down again and put her head in her hands. So far, coming home hadn't shaped up to be the lovefest she was promised. No, it was all yelling and screaming. She didn't know how much more of this she could take. She couldn't eat, couldn't sleep, couldn't work.

And nothing kept her from her relics. Winston, bless his uptight English soul, was working himself into an impressive strop just about every day, going on and on about 'those boys and their fraternity house malaise' and the 'Irish catastrophe' that was camping out on his beloved St. Augustine grass. And if she heard about the award-winning peonies one more time...well, you got three squares and cable in prison, right?

She sighed once more and went to the glass cabinet in the corner. Beneath the museum-quality lighting, a large, heavily decorated Egyptian death mask stared back at her, its inscrutable expression seeming to mock her. The gold and semi-precious stones gleamed with comforting warmth. She placed a loving hand on the glass. "I swear, Ahkenaten, you're the perfect man. You're rich. You're gorgeous." She laid her forehead on the glass and stared into its depths. "And you can't give me any lip."

Jude stood outside the door to the pool house, fist poised to knock on the door. It came as a surprise that he found himself here, preparing to seek comfort from the last person on his radar. He could easily have gone to Lucius or The Wonder Twins, but somehow he didn't think they would be able to help with his current predicament. Lucius had found the love of his life, and he and Persephone couldn't be happier. As for Mordecai and Elijah, they were closer than ever after what happened with Veronica and their confrontation with Lucifer. Any woman would be hard-pressed to come between them. He paused, but before he thought better of it, he knocked.

Domniel's reply was gruff. "What?"

"It's Jude. Can I come in?"

The door opened with a forceful *whoosh* of air, the action so fast it ruffled the grown-out locks that settled around the blind angel's face. Domniel looked like he felt. Like shit.

Domniel stepped aside and pulled the door open, allowing entry. Jude walked in a few steps, brushed his hand over the back of his head with a nervous swipe, and looked around. He didn't know what he expected Domniel's inner sanctuary to look like, but this wasn't it. It was clean and spartan, much like the room he had kept at the old place. From the erratic way his blind brother had been acting, he expected to see the turmoil in his soul reflected in his housekeeping. Not so.

Domniel crossed the floor and flopped down on the sofa with a surprising lack of grace. His movements were usually so careful and sure. "What do you want?"

Jude sat down in the opposite chair. "I don't know, I just thought we could talk about some things. We don't do that anymore. Haven't for a while, and I thought-"

"The redhead piss you off again?" Domniel interrupted, leaning back to cross his arms behind his head.

Jude laid his head back and stared at the ceiling, painted a bright blue with large puffy clouds. The effect was oddly pleasing. "It's a two-way street."

"Fuck her."

Jude snorted. "I thought we covered that."

Domniel shook his head, a soft chuckle spilling from his lips before his face hardened. "No, not 'fuck her'. Fuck. Her. Forget the bitch. You don't need her."

Jude's chest clenched at his brother's coldness. The cavalier attitude he was used to had morphed into something darker, more callous. "It's not that easy, Dom. I don't know what this is with me and Cori. It's--shit, I don't know. It's like there's something there. Or something could be there-"

His words cut off as Domniel shot forward, pinning him with what he knew was an icy glare behind the dark sunglasses. "Let's get this straight right now. I don't care. I don't care if you fuck her. I don't care if you don't. I don't care if you sit on the fence all day with your thumb up your ass, hemming and hawing about whether or not you want to fuck her. I don't care." He stood up and clenched his hands into fists at his side. "I. Don't. Fucking. Care. So do me a favor and take your whining, pansy ass back to Lucius. Bond over tea and cupcakes or something. Just get the fuck out and leave me alone."

Jude stared at him, open-mouthed, unable to process his brother's rant. His jaw snapped shut and he stood, spine straight. "Yeah," he managed. "I'll get out of your hair. Sorry to bother you."

Domniel said nothing and glared after him as he made his way to the door. As he closed it behind him, an overwhelming sense of sadness washed over him. Darkness was eating at his brother, like it was eating at all of them. Jude wondered what would happen when it finally devoured.

He walked from the pool house down the cobblestones that meandered about the grounds, taking his time and breathing in the fresh air. As he made his way further out, the vast landscape of the gardens came into view.

If there was one thing about Coriander's place that he liked, it had to be the gardens. Fragrant, lush, and expansive, they were a direct opposite to the tumultuous redhead. They were peaceful. Right now, he needed some peace. He strolled through, taking care not to deviate from the cobbled path, lest his footprints find their way back to Winston. The butler was overly fussy about his gardens, and a stray crushed blade of grass was sure to incur his wrath. He wanted to be able to eat breakfast without worrying about whether or not the prissy snot had spit in his coffee.

The path veered into a copse of stately magnolias alive with blooms, their soft scent permeating the air. A small, carved bench sat underneath the trees, looking out onto a sculpted row of flowerbeds, bursting with vibrancy. *Those must be the illustrious peonies.*

The worn wood of the bench creaked as he sat down, shifting to accommodate his size. He settled in, leaned his head back, and closed his eyes. He might as well give it another shot. Domniel had thrown him out, Lucius would patronize him, and Mordecai and Elijah wouldn't understand. Which left him with this last option if he was ever going to try to make sense of what was raging away beneath his skin.

Father, I need you. Please.

A soft breeze kicked up and blew across his face. Jude held his breath. Could it be? He waited, but all was silent. He exhaled slowly, feeling the air bleed out of his lungs.

Father. I was wrong. I need you.

The air stilled, yet the silence remained.

He sat forward with a jolt, despair creeping in to every corner of his heart. He looked out over the gardens, but there was nothing. No sound, no scent, nothing. As if time stood still and he was surrounded by it, suspended in the void. Nothing. He was alone.

Fuck it. Tears welled up in his eyes, and he choked down the crippling sob that threatened to burst forth. He tore out of the gardens on a run, not caring that his booted feet were ripping up grass and dirt, destroying the delicate foliage in his way. He had to get back to the house, back to his room. Somewhere he might find some salvation.

Later, as he watched his blood run in crimson rivers down the length of his body, he gave it one more try.

Father. Please.

When the silence became too much to bear, he dropped the knife and held a towel-wrapped fist to his mouth to scream, letting loose centuries-worth of pain. The silence still remained.

CHAPTER FOUR

He ached. Lucifer's joints protested as he eased himself up from the dirty floor into a sit, his naked legs flopping out in front of him as if they were boneless. He was caked in dirt and blood, along with a number of other bodily fluids he didn't want to acknowledge. His skin itched as the dried liquids cracked when he shifted, and his back burned under the strain of movement.

On impulse, he fluffed his wings out, but they were sluggish, as if hampered by weights. His eyes roved over the edges, ragged and torn, the once-beautiful appendages ugly in their disarray. At least they were still attached. He rubbed a grimy hand over his face, licking his lips against the dryness of his mouth, which tasted foul.

He had lost track of time since he had been pulled back from Switzerland, unsure of how long his Lord had been prolonging the torment. The Dark Lord's face, or at least what passed for one, had been angry and full of contempt. Apparently his ire had extended beyond the decimation of The Liar, and he had seen fit to unleash the rest of his irritation on Lucifer.

Lucifer's raspy chuckle was self-deprecating. He should have known he could not escape unscathed. It was only a matter of time before the hand that feeds would snap around and bite. And bite it did.

Twinges of pain skittered through his bones as he stood, looking out over the pile of bones and flesh in the dungeon. Someone else had been here with him. And yet, he was still alive. *Thank Heaven for small mercies.* He snorted at his own hubris, the insanity of his thought not lost on him.

Lucifer stepped forward and toed at a bloody femur in disgust. The air in the room rippled, growing warm as the scent of sulfur breached his nostrils. The pile of carnage disappeared, and the corner of the room transformed into a sunken bath, appointed with luxuries and fragrant with lavender and lemon.

A voice drifted in. *"You will be summoned to His presence soon, Morning Star. Prepare yourself."*

He told himself it was the desire to bathe and immerse his body in the decadent pool that had him scrambling in an uncharacteristic rush. It certainly wasn't the sliver of fear that snaked down his spine.

"Ah, there you are, Morning Star. How lovely you come."

The words rolled over Lucifer in a sinuous whisper. He bowed low with sincere deference. "As You please, my Lord." He fingered the edge of the black cloak. "You honor me with such finery. How may I serve?"

"We trust you understand that We could not let your part in The Liar's failure go unpunished?" Satan's voice held no sympathy.

Lucifer's jaw clenched as his stomach rolled over. The Liar had failed by her own hand; he had merely delivered the assignment. He bowed again. "Of course, my Lord," he said smoothly, tinging the words with submission. "You are possessed of infinite patience. I thank You for Your graciousness."

"Yes, well, We are giving you another opportunity to prove your worth to Us." The imperious tone set Lucifer's teeth on edge. "You will go to The Dealer. We feel his skillset will be what is required for the next step in Our plan." An envelope appeared in the air in front of him, and he took it between his fingers, tucking it away in the cloak. "Deliver the assignment to The Dealer. Make him understand the urgency of Our request. Assist him as required."

Another deep bow. "Of course, my Lord. I am ever Your tool. Is that all?"

Satan's eyes burned with a deep yellow fire. "No. The Catalyst still lives, and We still have need of her. Keep watch on her and report back to Us."

"Certainly, my Lord."

"There is one other thing, Morning Star. The Incubus."

The cold fear was back, trickling down his spine. The damned thing would be the death of him. If he was lucky. "What of him?"

"You seem to have some trouble keeping him to his place. He is somehow able to come and go at will. Secure him at all costs. We will not have him spreading his demon seed across Our world. We will chain him to you if you cannot contain him."

"I understand, my Lord. I shall not fail You."

"See that you don't."

The dismissal was obvious. Lucifer bowed for the last time, turned and left. He could feel the heat from the envelope seeping into his skin, the weight of the cloak pressing it into his body. With a loud crack he was gone, eager to rid himself of the missive and of his Lord's domain.

The tiny overhead bell tinkled merrily as Lucifer opened the door and stepped inside. The antiques shop was quaint and dusty, rife with the smell of ancient things, yet his nose detected an undercurrent of something more familiar.

"How may I be of--ah, it's you." The Dealer emerged from a curtained partition, the genial smile on his face falling as his eyes recognized his patron. "What brings you here, Lucifer?"

Lucifer's hand produced the envelope. "Our Lord has need of you, " his eyes flicked to take in the brass nameplate by the point-of-sale register on the counter, *"Reginald."*

The Dealer eyed the envelope with a raised eyebrow. He reached out to take it, and Lucifer noticed the slight tremor to his fingers. It seemed he wasn't the only one affected by the weight of duty. "And what is required of me, that you deliver his message in person?"

"I do as I am commanded, same as you."

The Dealer's smile was cold. "Of course." He ripped open the envelope and scanned the missive. His eyes widened and an arched eyebrow rose in speculation. "The Finder? Well, that does make things interesting. It would seem His Grace knows to whom he should turn." He refolded the note and tucked it away in his jacket. "Were you aware of this?" He gestured to the hidden envelope.

"No," Lucifer murmured. "I was not privy to that information."

"Really?" The Dealer grinned. "Most interesting."

Lucifer pulled himself straight and narrowed his gaze. "I presume I don't need to tell you what will happen if you fail? After The Liar fucked it up, I must say he's downright peevish, and further disappointments will be just as ugly."

Blue eyes raked over him with an unsettling perusal. "Yes, I heard." The haughty sniff was laced with derision. "I never liked her, anyway. Good riddance. I see you remain unblemished, though. A little tired around the eyes." A simpering smile worked its way across The Dealer's thin lips. "Perhaps some fresh air might do you good, Lucifer. I hear Switzerland is lovely this time of year."

The jab was blatant and twisted in his belly. Of course it was known how he had been dragged back in disgrace. Lucifer's fingers twitched with the urge to set the smug bastard's face on fire. He refrained, pleased with the level of restraint he was able to muster.

"Do not fail, Reginald. That is all." Lucifer turned on his heel and left before the last of his self-control wavered. If the Dark Lord wanted his head, he certainly wasn't going to lose it over a peon like Reginald. Ruffled pride somewhat soothed, he set off to complete the rest of his tasks. Perhaps The Incubus would bear the brunt of his irritation once he caught up to him. Yes, that would please him. He sighed and carded a hand through his platinum locks, enjoying the burst of lavender and lemon that lingered. Yes, he was feeling much better already.

The night air was cool, and a northerly breeze drifted in, ruffling the escaped tendrils of hair from her ponytail. The roof of her house was flat in one area for a reason, accessible by a hidden staircase on the third floor that only a few knew about. When a scuffling off to her left caught her attention, she smiled.

"You can come on out, Sephie, I know it's you."

Persephone scrambled up the ladder from the third floor balcony and crawled onto the roof. "How did you know it was me?"

Coriander held her hand out and waited for her sister to reach her. "Because Winston knows better than to bother me up here unless there's an emergency, and I didn't hear Teir and her noisy bells. Who else could it be?"

Persephone's smile was soft. "I don't know. Jude, maybe?"

She snorted. "Right. Like he would be caught dead up here with me. I don't think either of us could control the urge to throw someone off."

"He's hurting, Cori." Persephone snuggled up next to her, and Coriander threw an arm around her.

"We all have our hurts, Sephie. Some of us are just better at dealing with them."

Persephone leaned in. "Are we okay? You and me? I mean, when you left before. We've never fought like that. Ever."

Coriander squeezed and thought for a moment. Were they okay? The hard knot of betrayal she felt seemed to have melted away, leaving behind a bitter ache. Was it the betrayal that lingered, or regret for her actions? Persephone's face was open and earnest, and it warmed her heart in an old, familiar way. "Yeah, girly," she sighed, resting her head on Persephone's. "We're good." She chuckled. "No more making friends with stray hookers, okay?"

Her sister's soft laugh echoed in the moonlight. "Well, how was I supposed to know she was a demon interested in bleeding me dry? She wasn't exactly forthcoming with that bit of information, you know. It was more of a live and learn process."

Coriander pulled back, staring into Persephone's face with concern. "What did happen, Seph? I mean, are you okay? Really okay? What did she do to you?"

Persephone shrugged. "It's still a little fuzzy. She drugged me. With Teir's good Irish Breakfast, no less." Her blond head shook as she laughed. "Waste of a perfectly good 'cuppa'."

Coriander swallowed hard against the lump in her throat. It was so like Persephone to make light of the situation. "Be serious, you."

"I am. Like I said, she drugged me, and we were looking into this mirror we had bought for her bedroom." Persephone's face lit up. "Oh, Cori! You would have loved this mirror! We picked it up in this great little antiques store in town. There were all sorts of things that you would just love. We should go. Anyway, we were standing in front of the mirror, and I think we were sucked into another dimension or circle of Hell or something…"

Coriander's brain misfired the second her sister uttered the word 'mirror'. Mirrors were often powerful artifacts, and if this demon knew where to get a mirror that would do exactly what Persephone had described, then what else waited at this shop?

"Sephie," she interrupted, "I think that's a great idea. We'll go shopping." She turned her sister in her arms and stared into her face. "Hey, I just want to tell you that I'm sorry." Coriander paused, taking a moment to smooth the hair back from Persephone's face. "I mean it. I'm sorry we fought like that. I was angry and stupid. I was hurting and chose to lash out at you instead of talking it out. I said cruel things that I didn't mean." She tucked her bottom lip between her teeth in embarrassment. "I love you, I hope you know that. And I'm so sorry."

Persephone's eyes welled up with tears, and she stifled back a sob as she pulled Coriander into her arms. "I'm sorry too, sis. And I forgive you. I love you."

Coriander melted into the comfort of Persephone's embrace and felt a small part of her heart rejoice at the acceptance. Everything was right again.

The tiny bell over the door tinkled as Coriander and Persephone made their way inside, the musty smell of old things permeating the air in a comforting perfume. Coriander breathed deeply and sighed with a wistful smile.

"Told you," Persephone said, beaming at her sister.

"So you did."

The door shut softly behind them, eliciting another small peal of the bell. The shop was littered with pieces from floor to ceiling, a jumble of furnishing and accessories displayed in a careful array of ordered chaos. There was much to see.

"Oh, Cori!" Persephone gasped, grabbing her arm and ushering her over to a collection of ancient trunks. "Look at these! Aren't these beautiful?"

"Yes." The word came out in a rush of air as Coriander bent to inspect one of the larger trunks. It was solid, handcrafted from old woods, and held together by a series of ornate steel strappings. The dark stain was rich, the color of Turkish coffee, and the polished wood gleamed. Thick brass rivets were hammered into the filigreed steel bindings, and the large latches on the front were shiny and beautiful. Her fingers twitched at her side, and before she knew it, her hands came up to touch, running over the trunk in a whisper of reverence.

"It's a beautiful piece, isn't it?" A voice said smoothly from behind her. "I picked it up in Kusadasi along with a lovely armoire. It is rumored to have come from Topkapi Palace, from the apartments of the Queen Mother. I paid handsomely for it. But for the right price, it could be yours."

Coriander straightened and turned to the man. He was tall, elegantly so, dressed in a tweed suit that screamed 'Savile Row'. The smile he gave her was warm and polished, gleaming much like the teak wood of the trunk. He wore a pair of thin, wire-rimmed glasses that perched on the end of an aristocratic nose. Cool eyes behind the frames assessed her with a prodding gaze.

"It's lovely," she managed after a moment. "And if you can prove its origin, I would say you have a sale."

He laughed, more of a warm chuckle than a true laugh, and said, "Alas, it is only rumor, my dear. But the beauty of the piece speaks for itself." His hand swept the air in a grand gesture. "And I do have many more pieces with confirmed provenance that might hold your interest, Miss—?"

"Coriander Rhodes," she supplied, holding out her hand. "And you, sir?"

The handshake was strong, yet not too tight. Friendly. "Ah, where are my manners, Miss Rhodes? Do forgive me. Reginald Wickham-Jones, at your service." He gave a polite, deferential bow. "Now, are you in the market for anything in particular?"

Coriander smiled and let her gaze wander. She could hear Persephone in another corner of the shop fawning over something. "I'm a bit of a collector. Usually Middle Eastern and Egyptian. I'm currently harboring an obsession for anything Eighteenth Dynasty."

"Really? How interesting. I have recently come into possession of a fragmented quartzite statuary piece of Meketaten. Would you be interested?"

Coriander's mind reeled as she thought back to the death mask in her office. A statue of one of Akhenaten's daughters? She buzzed with excitement. "I would definitely be interested," she replied.

"Come with me." He turned and gestured for her to follow.

Coriander shot back over her shoulder, "Be right back, Seph! Don't wander off." She listened for the distant reply and followed Reginald into another room of the shop. As she passed through the colorful silk fabric of the room divider, a shiver tickled at the back of her mind. She couldn't forget Persephone's mirror. While her sister's ordeal was terrifying and supernatural, she wondered how much of it had been the work of Veronica, and how much had been the mirror itself.

Reginald stood in the far back of the room next to a wooden packing crate. He smiled as she moved closer. "I must say, I have been debating whether or not I wanted to sell this particular piece or keep it for my personal collection." The lines of his kind face grew deeper as his smile widened. "But I see fate has had a hand in my decision by bringing me a kindred spirit."

He picked up the crowbar from the floor and wedged it under the lid of the crate. The wood creaked as he pried the lid open. The scent of sand and straw assaulted her and immediately brought her mind back to Egypt. Reginald's hands were sure and steady as he removed the lid and set it aside. A large, wrapped bundle lay nestled in the straw, and she couldn't help but hold her breath as Reginald gingerly picked up the object.

It lay in the crook of his arms, as one would hold an infant, and he smiled up at her with the same beatific expression of a new parent. "Would you like to do the honors?"

She nodded, unable to speak, emotion and excitement lodging in her throat. Coriander's hands were still with years of experience at handling fragile objects, but she was nervous just the same. This was a huge find and she knew it. All she had to do was unwrap it.

Coriander's fingers curled around the soft cloth, peeling it back on a breath. It was beautiful. Fragmented indeed, as it was missing the head and part of the hand. The hieroglyphics carved at the bottom revealed that it was in fact, Meketaten.

"It's her," Coriander whispered, trailing a hand over the carved script. "*Protected by Aten*," she translated the name. Her eyes shot up to Reginald. "Whatever you want, I'll pay it. I have to have her."

Reginald returned her smile and replaced the statue. "I think we'll be able to reach an agreement. I'm glad she will be going to someone who will appreciate her beauty." He returned the lid to the crate and gestured to the door. "Shall we negotiate?"

Coriander followed him to the front and found Persephone standing by the counter. "Did you find something?" Persephone asked. "I knew you would."

Reginald took his place behind the counter and pulled out a notepad and pen. He scribbled for a moment and slid the pad across the counter. "If you find this sum agreeable, Miss Rhodes?"

Coriander looked down at the pad. She paused for a moment and then took the pen from his grasp. She drew a line through the figure and jotted down a new one beneath it. There was a glint in her eye as she passed the pad back to Reginald. This was a dance with which she was familiar, one that started the blood rushing in her veins. The find may not have been hers, but she was fairly sure she would take home the spoils.

Reginald's eyebrow rose at Coriander's figure, and for a second she feared he would turn her down. She waited and watched as the corners of his lips turned up into a slight smile. He raised his eyes to hers. "She's worth so much more, you know. And you drive a hard bargain," he said, offering her his hand. "But you have a deal."

Coriander met his grip with a firm shake. "If you'll give me the account details, I'll have it wired over to you as soon as possible, then we can arrange delivery."

"Very good." Reginald plucked one of his business cards from the counter and turned it over to scrawl a series of numbers on the back. "Your accountant should find everything in order for the transfer. Ring me if you have any other questions or issues."

Coriander took the card. "I'll be in touch soon. Thank you."

Reginald gave a slight bow at the waist. "The pleasure was mine. You ladies are welcome anytime. Who knows what treasures find their way here?"

She grabbed Persephone and nodded as they made their way out. Once outside, Persephone spun her around. "So, what did you buy?"

"A statue."

Persephone's face was flush with excitement. "A statue? That's all you have to say? Most of the time I have to tune you out when you start talking about your relics."

Coriander wrinkled her nose. "Well, that's not nice. Don't tell me that."

Persephone laughed as she linked their arms together and started walking. "I still love you, though."

She squeezed Coriander's arm. "How much was that thing, anyway?"

"A quarter mil."

"What?" Persephone squeaked. "You spent two-hundred and fifty-thousand dollars on a statue?"

Coriander threw her head back and laughed with gusto. "Two words, Sephie. Egyptian. Princess."

The Dealer flipped the sign on the window and returned to the counter, quickly going through the end of day procedure. Once the tediousness had been dealt with, he opened a drawer to the left of the register, pulling out a ballpoint pen. He set it on the counter and stared at it for a moment, a small, satisfied smile creeping across his features. It was the last thing she had touched, and he had squirreled it away, careful to ensure no other customer handled the writing instrument.

He closed his eyes, laid his hands on the counter, palms down, and blew out a deep breath. He counted to ten and reached out, curling his fingers around the tiny cylinder of plastic. Images assailed him as he opened up his mind, seeking the essence the red-headed woman had left behind. They filed past in a shuffle, a disjointed cinema in flashes of bright color. He saw sand and never-ending dunes, pyramids and tombs, wonders of worlds lost, and treasures too numerous to count.

He shuddered and leaned forward as male faces came into view, all of them terrifyingly familiar, save one. Concentrating, he paused on the image of the dark-haired man. Tall and tanned, with a whiplash smile, the man exuded confidence and the easy grace of privilege. Blue light swirled around him, causing The Dealer to gasp in alarm. An Anubis. In the flesh. Dangerous and interesting. He filed that away for later perusal and continued on.

A few glimpses later, he slowed the procession again, this time peering harder into the vision. An office. Her office, judging by the wall-to-wall library shelving and the number of artifacts ensconced in display cases. A tongue swiped out over his lips, feeling the need to wet a mouth suddenly gone dry. Staring back at him from behind glass was a perfectly preserved Egyptian death mask. Akhenaten. Yes, this he could work with.

The cool golden and inlaid visage slipped past, and the next image that came forth made him stop breathing altogether. The tall man was back, his hand wrapped around a smaller one. One that belonged to a little girl. Her long red hair and bright green eyes were a carbon copy of the woman who had been in his shop not hours before. A daughter. A treasure above all others. But she was not the treasure his Lord was after.

A few more images later, what he sought finally came into view. There on a bookshelf, under an inconspicuous glass case, lay the artifact in question. A small obsidian stone, fashioned onto a gold chain. The image was not perfectly clear, but there was no doubt this was it. It was smooth, worn down by centuries of touch, the inscriptions barely visible.

On a broken gasp, The Dealer let go of the pen and opened his eyes. The irises glowed with an intense yellow fire, and his lips curled back in a feral snarl. He would procure the object, but he would bring back more. Surely, his Lord would not object to some forward thinking on his part? After all, it was no secret that Lucifer had been disappointing as of late, and anything he could do to get into his Lord's good graces would not be amiss.

Lucifer. The snarl on his lips deepened and a small growl escaped in a huff of breath. The arrogant tosser deserved everything he got. He was as cold as he was beautiful, icy and untouchable. As sharp as he was dangerous. The favorite flavor of the past millennia. It was enough to make his stomach turn.

The Dealer pulled open the drawer and retrieved his missive. He stared down at the envelope his visitor had left and smiled, remembering the distaste plastered across Lucifer's smooth features. How interesting that the fallen angel's name, once whispered in reverent tones, now sparked him to a satisfying smirk of pity. Lucifer, the blindingly beautiful angel who once ushered the downfall of Heaven's greatest angels with his silver tongue, reduced to delivering lower-level missions by hand. The smirk widened to a grin. Satan's personal postman in a three-piece suit.

And now the opportunity he'd waited for was handed over by the best-dressed lackey in the Nine circles. Growing ambition coiled in his belly. His orders were clear. But there was nothing said about going above and beyond this dark call of duty. He thought about the redhead and her treasures. Oh, yes. Not only would he succeed, but he would triumph on unheard of levels. The envelope crumpled in his hand. And wouldn't that just take the shine off the Morning Star's designer shoes?

CHAPTER FIVE

Coriander shut Ashtiru's door behind her with a soft click. A flicker of movement to her left made her turn. Alex stood in the shadows of the long hallway, the light from the open door of the bedroom spilling over the crossed arms over his chest.

"She asleep?"

"Of course she is. Teir and Seph had her running all over the yard all afternoon," she replied. "The child was exhausted."

The long line of Alex's body shifted into a casual lean against the door frame. It made him look inviting, and the bastard knew it. That was the problem with Alex. He knew exactly how to use his appeal to his advantage. If she were still in love with him, it would be annoying. Now it was just tiring.

"Come inside? Have a drink?" he asked quietly.

Why the hell not? Even if it was his room, it was still her house. She nodded and swept past him. His bedroom was one of the few in the house she rarely entered. It was as permanent a place as it could be for him, especially when they juggled their parental duties. Coriander wanted them to be together as much as possible when she and Alex weren't working, so it seemed to make sense to give the man his own space in a bedroom next to their daughter's. Christ knew she had enough room.

Alex turned and shut the door, smirking at her raised eyebrow. "Oh, calm down. I've no intention of trying to seduce you." His teeth flashed in a quick grin. "Unless you want me to."

"Subtle."

"I try." He went to the little cabinet in the corner of the room and pulled out two glasses and, pouring them both a drink. "Here," he said, handing her the glass. "Drink that and tell me about your shopping trip. Your sister said something about a statue."

Coriander took the glass and sat down on the edge of the bed, the fingers of her other hand picking imaginary fluff off the duvet. The steel-gray duponi was pebbled beneath her fingertips, and she let them drag across the silk without thought. She raised her head to look at his face. In the dim light of his room, his eyes were almost the color of the bedspread. Winston's doing, no doubt. The butler would have ensured Alex's room was as tailored to him as possible.

"It was a good find," she said, watching him move to stand with his back against the wall. She frowned. "Do you have something against the furniture in my house? You seem to do nothing but drape yourself in doorways."

A long fingered hand raised the glass to his lips, and he smiled at her over the rim of the crystal tumbler. She watched his throat bob as he swallowed a mouthful of scotch. "I've always been a bit of leaner, you know that." His smile softened as he lowered the glass. "We used to lean on each other."

Coriander sighed, wanting to close her eyes against the truth contained in his words. Instead, she stared into the amber depths of her glass. "We still do, just...not like that anymore."

"I've noticed."

"You said you weren't going to do this," she countered, irritation stiffening her spine.

"This isn't seduction, Coriander," Alex huffed. "You've made your thoughts clear on that."

"Then what are you doing?" she hissed.

"Maybe I want more."

She barked out a harsh laugh, but controlled herself at the raise of his eyebrow and jerk of his head toward Ashtiru's room. She shook her head. "No, you don't. You haven't wanted that for a long time." Her eyes bore into his, and his challenging glare made her burn. "Admit it, the only reason you're talking about this is because you think I'm interested in someone else."

"Aren't you?" She couldn't ignore the bite to his tone.

"What does it matter, Alex? We admitted it wouldn't work between us. Hell, we weren't even together when I got pregnant with Ash. It was a last-ditch drunken hot mess of a mistake."

His eyes narrowed and he leaned forward, muscles tight with a slight menace. "Are you saying Ash — ?"

"Don't be stupid," she snapped. "And don't put words in my mouth. Ash is not the mistake. Thinking we could try to fix it was the mistake. And if she's the reason we came together that last time, fine, I can reconcile that. For fuck's sake, I can rejoice in that. She was meant to be. Not the rest of it. It won't ever happen again," she said with conviction. "Ever."

"You don't mean th — "

She cut him off with her hand. "I do mean that. I love you," she said on a sigh. "I will always love you. You are the father of my child, and I will never begrudge you that or try to keep you away from her. But we are done. You do things — you take risks that I can't. And I can't be there for you because I have to be there for her. One of us has to always come home."

"Says the woman who plunders caves in the heart of the Iraqi insurgency," he shot back.

Coriander's eyes flashed as she sneered, "At least I'm not the one trying to dick over the Sunnis and the Shiites at the same time." It tugged at her heart to hear the hurt in his voice, but she couldn't go on like this. "Look, we could argue about this from now until the end of time. I made my choice. You're going to have to live with it."

"And that's what you chose? What did you call him? Ah, yes, 'a drunken pigeon'?" He took another gulp from the glass. "Sounds like a winner, dear. You sure know how to pick 'em."

She leaped to her feet, thrusting a finger at him. The jerky movement sent scotch splashing out of the glass and over her hand. She paid it no mind and curled her lip at him. "Don't," she warned. "Don't start something that you will regret. I meant what I said, I won't keep you from Ash, but don't make me let you go this way."

Alex pushed off the wall and moved to stand over her. He was more than a head taller, but his height had never fazed her. She glared up at him and met his narrowed gaze.

"What did you expect me to say?" he growled. "Did you think I would just roll over and play dead for you while you fall into bed with someone else?"

She poked a finger in his chest and he frowned, his hand coming up to rub the injured spot. "No. This is not about me and sex. I've been with others since we split up, and so have you. This is about Jude and whatever you think is going on. Your problem isn't with me. It's with him."

Alex grunted and stepped back, his features twisting into a mask of emotion she had only seen twice in their years together. His hand came up and she saw his knuckles tighten around the glass.

"You throw that glass, and I swear on Zeus' flaming balls I will kick your lanky Greek ass from here to Crete and drown you in the Mediterranean." Her voice held an undercurrent of violence she knew he would understand.

They both went stiff, each waiting for the other to breathe, when finally Alex blinked and handed her the glass without a word. He turned away from her face and mumbled under his breath.

"What was that?" she asked.

Alex's dark curls hung over his face as he looked back over his shoulder. "He will not replace me."

Coriander's breath came out in a rush. That's what this was about? She never imagined that Alex could see it that way. "You're her father. You will always be her father. No one can replace you in her heart."

He turned to face her, and she could see every emotion within him plastered on the smooth, tanned skin of his face. His eyes burned with want, love, need, and fear.

His voice registered barely above a whisper. "What about yours?"

There was so much she wanted to say to him. After all, they shared a child and a past, and were looking down the long road of a future of some sort. She wanted to tell him that things would work out the way they should, give him every insipid platitude she learned from Persephone. Some hope of...something. In the end, all she could manage was a broken, "I'm sorry."

"No, you're not." His voice was like ice, cold and cutting, straight to her heart.

"I am," she replied. "But if you keep this shit up, you'll never get to understand how much I mean it. And that's your loss, Alex." She pushed past him and set both glasses on the dresser by the door. She faced him one last time as she yanked open the bedroom door. "You can either make your peace or burn your bridges. Whatever you decide is on your head, not mine."

Jude looked up from the book he was reading as Coriander high-tailed it down the stairs and across the living room to her office, slamming the door behind her so hard it rattled. A sigh filtered down from above, and his gaze looked up to see Alex's drawn face staring down at him. The dark-haired man said nothing, but walked down the stairs and out the front door without a backward glance. Jude set his book down and followed after Coriander.

He turned the knob and walked in slowly, half-expecting a projectile to come sailing through the air. She stood at the far end of her office, looking out of the glass panes of the French doors, arms crossed over her chest in a protective gesture.

"Did he leave?" Her voice wavered.

"Out the front door. But not for good, I don't think."

"Good. He's got some things he needs to rethink before he darkens my door again."

"And what about you? Are you blameless in whatever's going on between the two of you?"

She whirled around to face him, fire blazing in her eyes. "There's nothing going on between the two of us. Something neither he nor you can seem to get through your thick skulls. It's tiring, Jude. So fucking tiring."

"What about Ash?" he asked, knowing that bringing her up was a powder keg waiting to happen.

"What about her? She stays in Greece with Alex's parents at a lovely villa in Mykonos, thank you very much, when she can't be with us. She knows I love her, and she knows he loves her. That's all that matters. God knows that's all that matters to me."

"What do you know about God, Coriander?" Jude snorted. "You're no bastion of piety."

"I don't need to be. Because every time I look into the face of that little girl, I want to fall to my knees to bask in the grace I see in her eyes. She is the best thing that has ever happened to me. I see it. I feel it. It's divine. You can't convince me otherwise. Have a little faith. Remember that everything in this life has a purpose. Whether you realize it or not."

Bitter emotion swallowed the fallen angel. *I wish I could, Coriander. I wish I could.*

"You, of all people, are telling me to have faith? Faith in what? Don't you get it? He's gone. From me." Jude beat at his chest. "He's gone from me. He speaks to Lucius. But not to me." He snorted, his face twisting into a cruel sneer. "Faith. That's rich coming from a woman who blunders her way through life with a dog and a bastard. That's not faith, that's luck."

Coriander's face was hard. "You should watch your mouth. I'm somebody's mother, remember?"

No shit. The look on Coriander's face was a sucker punch to the gut. He'd crossed a line and he knew it the minute the words flew out of his damned mouth. Jude opened his mouth to apologize and actually mean it, when Coriander shoved a finger in his face.

"Just so we're clear, big guy, if I ever hear you shoot your mouth off like that again about my child, I will break you. There won't be enough left for even The Almighty to put to rights. And then I will make sure you spend eternity in my backyard pooper-scooping for the Anubis. Got it?"

"Yeah, I got it," he said, running a hand over the back of his head. "So what do you and the Anubis get up to in your jaunts across the globe?"

The smile that spread across her face was blinding. "Let me show you." She walked over to her desk and picked up a small duffel that sat on the floor next to it. She placed it on the desktop and rummaged through the contents. He walked over and peered inside.

It was bigger than it looked, and he could see books and two spiral-bound notebooks, along with some small scroll tubes. He looked back over the desktop and his eyes rested on the little brass business card holder. He wondered why he hadn't seen it before as he picked up one of the cards. It was a heavy cream cardstock, her name printed in bold block letters.

Coriander Rhodes, Salvage and Reclamation.

He held the card up for her to see. "I thought you were a doctor?"

She snorted as she unpacked the duffel. "I am. I'm a history professor. So's Alex. That's how we met, at the University of Athens."

"What, like Indiana Jones?"

"Not quite," she frowned. "He's fictional. And I don't carry a whip or wear a jaunty hat."

He flipped the card over in his hands. "But this says-"

"Those aren't my teaching credentials, Jude. It's what I do. What we do when we're not in the classroom. We find things. Ancient places, lost places, relics, religions, civilizations. Life," she stressed. "People. It's amazing work."

He gazed at the card again before turning cold eyes on her. "And then you sell it to the highest bidder."

Her jaw clenched and her eyebrow went up. "No. I don't deal on the black market. Alex may dabble, but that's his gamble. The laws are very clear about that sort of thing, and the prison system over there isn't the five-star affair like it is here in the States, nor is it worth the massive amount of cash I would have to throw away to steer clear of it. I like hanging onto my hands and my money."

"But he takes risks," Jude pressed.

"We both do, to some extent. These things belong to the world. It's a sacrilege to let them wither away and die under the sand, or in some Saudi prince's private collection that he nicked without the proper paperwork. Those things, we find. We find, and we get them back. A lot of these antiquities are hidden away on yachts that keep to international waters. That's Alex's specialty."

Jude's eyes widened as he dropped the card onto the desk with a splutter. "Pirates. You're talking about pirates, aren't you? That's what Alex does in his spare time, right? He's a fucking pirate! That's why you let Ash stay with his parents? Because Long John Silver isn't home long enough to be a father to his little girl?"

She pretended to ignore him, continuing to rifle through her bag.

"Coriander?"

She flinched at his tone and whipped her head up. "Nobody said anything about," her fingers shot up to make air quotes, "pirates."

"Then how do you define men with large quantities of firearms on the open sea ambushing unsuspecting vessels?"

She wrinkled her nose. "It's all subjective. Those idiots off the coast of Africa, yeah, they're pirates. But what Alex does, it's...he's," she paused, frustrated. "It's just different, okay? He knows what he's doing and makes sure no one gets hurt. Pirate is such an ugly word. Try, 'nautical acquisition and redistribution specialist'." She shook her head and went back to the bag, muttering, "I mean, really, it's not nearly as nefarious as you make it sound." She shoved at the bag and jerked her head up to face him, the scowl covering the whole of her face. "And why do you care in the first place?"

"Because it's wrong, Coriander. You can put a pig in a tutu and put it on stage, but it will never be a ballerina," he frowned.

Her brow lifted in confusion. "What in the hell does that mean? Have you been watching Dr. Phil reruns again?"

He grabbed her arm and yanked her around the edge of the desk, hauling her against the wall of his chest. "It means, no matter how prettily you choose to define it, it is what it is."

His mouth went dry as the pain in his soul receded, and something low stirred in his groin, burning beautifully as he felt her breath on his face.

"And what is it?" she asked, her lips parting.

His eyes darkened to slits as his mouth slowly descended. A second before they made contact, he whispered, "Wrong."

Her mouth was soft and wet, and opened like a flower unfurling into the sunlight. Warmth, precious and cradling, enveloped him as he angled his head to plunder the depths of her mouth. Coriander made a small gasping sound as his tongue snaked out to tangle with hers. The breathy noise went straight to his cock, making him hard in an instant. His hands pressed their way up her arms, sliding over skin like silk, to cup the back of her head and hold her in place while his mouth ground over hers.

She sagged against him, winding her arms around his waist for support, and pressed her body to his. His back lit up like Christmas, the tattoo of his wings burning so hot, he swore it would set the fabric of his t-shirt alight. Coriander gave as good as she got, returning the kiss with equal pressure, her tongue demanding in its own right. Her mouth moved with purpose, each sweep of her tongue and slick slide of her lips seeking out the recesses of his mouth, learning every secret spot as she attacked it with fervor.

Desire, thick and rich, shivered out over his skin, coating him in want. It was only a kiss, and yet it was so much more. A harbinger of pleasures to come, the curtain call on this dance they had shared, a promise ready to be fulfilled.

She pulled back, panting against his open mouth. "Upstairs. Now."

Jude released her and she grabbed his hand, leading him out of the office and through the living room. He had eyes for nothing else except Coriander, his vision trained on the line of her back as she strode in front of him. She pulled him up the stairs in silence to the second floor and down the hall to her bedroom at the end. The instant they were inside, he kicked the door shut and spun her around to pin her against it.

The taste of her hit his tongue and he groaned, rubbing his hands over her body, kneading and squeezing any soft skin he came across. Her head fell back against the door and she moaned; a low sound full of want as he bent to latch on to her neck. She arched into him like an offering, and he murmured his approval against her collarbone.

Her hands came up to catch at his scalp, her short nails digging in with tiny stings. The sensation was thrilling, and he clung to her for more. She allowed him a few more seconds of worship at her neck before her tiny hands pushed him off and spun him to reverse their positions.

She licked her lips and grabbed the waistband of his jeans. There was no warning as Coriander jerked the fly open and pulled the zipper down fast enough that it abraded the underside of his cock. He hissed through gritted teeth at the burn, and looked down just in time to realize that the hand that grasped him tightly had no intention of letting go. Her eyes rolled to meet his briefly before she turned her full attention back to his erection. She gave it a rough squeeze, her hand sliding up the shaft as her pert red tongue licked the tip.

The moan that rumbled from his chest was feral, vibrating across his skin. Leaning in, she teased him as she grazed her teeth across the head, eliciting another hiss from his lips. The waiting was driving him crazy. Finally, he ripped of the tie of her ponytail and tangled his hands in the locks of the soft auburn hair, growling, "Do it."

As Coriander leaned in to suck on the head of his cock, Jude tightened his grip in her hair, urging her with gentle pressure to take more. Coriander recoiled as she struggled to take it all in. He eased back, letting her relax, but the feel of her mouth around him was too much, and he had to have more. He pulled out so that only the sensitive head was in her mouth before aggressively thrusting the full length back in, using the grip on her hair to hold her in the position he wanted.

She sucked hard as he thrust in, and bit down as he pulled out, her teeth sharply raking his entire length from base to head. Jude hissed, "Yes," ramming his cock back into the hot, tight depth of her mouth.

She was driving him insane. The pressure of her mouth as she sucked, and her teeth as they bit, were causing only a tease of the ecstasy he knew was coming. Every thrust in, Jude could feel her throat muscles working around his cock, squeezing like a vice. He pulled back out, her teeth scraping his entire length. Each thrust was harder than the previous until the feel of her short, well-manicured nails digging into his balls brought him to the edge. Looking down at her through the haze of his lust, the struggle to keep him buried to the base in her mouth was evident.

Jude wanted more. Needed more. With a growl, he pulled his cock completely from her mouth to chuck the remainder of his clothes. When he was naked before her, he pulled her up and stripped her with haste. There would be time to savor her body once he got her on the bed.

Coriander was pulling great gulps of air as he picked her up and carried her to the bed, tossing her down to cover her body with his. Their mouths met in a furious tangle of lips, tongue, and teeth, wet and needy.

She tasted light and sweet, like the warm winds of summer as he kissed her. At some point in the kiss her arms stretched up, fingers digging into his hair and pulling until he felt his scalp burn. She returned the kiss with a hunger that Jude met with fierce intensity. Still engrossed in the taste of her mouth, he leaned down and cupped the delicious roundness of her ass, using it to lift her up.

Instinctively, Coriander wrapped her firm legs around him, allowing Jude to impale her on his rampant erection. He broke the kiss, crying out as she seated onto his cock and dug her nails into shoulders. Wings, long gone, flexed as though to cradle her body as she hissed at his girth stretching her. It could have been pleasure, it could have been pain; she was so small and tight around him. She leaned her head in, her lips mouthing against his collarbone. She was tight around his cock and Jude moaned as he thrust, the feel of her body searing off any other thought in his brain.

He bucked, pushing her further into the mattress, each slam forcing her body to take more of him. She tensed against him, her soft gasps turning to harsh grunts against his skin. He was taking more of her, his body requiring it, needing her wrapped around him, needing to fill her. The urge was primal and fierce, and his body moved to sate it.

Jude cried out in ecstasy as she sank her teeth into his shoulder, breaking skin. Those perfect little white teeth, usually flashing her little fox grin, bit down even harder. It spurred him to thrust hard enough that she let go of his shoulder to cry out, her pain and pleasure echoing in his ears. Coriander felt so good that Jude wasn't sure if he could last. This was home. Her body was as close to Heaven as he figured he was ever going to get, and Jude went after those gates with a battering ram.

Every cry was his choir, every shudder was another rumble of the Voice, and every touch of breath on his skin was the kiss of God. This woman was his world, and he knew if she didn't take everything he had to give, his world was going to come crashing down.

It was only then he paused. He reached up behind her and grabbed a pillow. He wrapped an arm around her legs and lifted the lower half of her body. With a grunt, he shoved the pillow under her ass, arching her body up a little more. He missed the flash of concern in her eyes as he locked rough hands onto her thighs and rammed his cock back in full force at the new angle. Her cry was high and stuttered, and she stilled.

Jude moaned as he kept going. He was so lost to his need that for a moment he didn't notice that Coriander wasn't moving. When he looked down, Jude's eyes met hers and his heart stopped. Fat tears slid from the corners of her bright jade eyes, her pain beating at him in silence. With a dawning horror, he realized that he'd crossed the line and gone way too far. She deserved so much better than what he'd given her. Carefully, so not to hurt her worse, Jude slowly withdrew from her body and rolled back onto his knees, looking down at her.

"I-Oh, God, Cori-"

She reached for him with a shaky hand. "Easy there, tiger. You break it, you bought it."

She was breathtaking, even as tears glittered in her eyes. Jude's eyes drank in the sight of her spread before him and his chest felt hot and heavy with how badly he wanted to drown in the woman before him. From the moment they met, she had been a tidal wave coming down on him, and Jude no longer wanted to run for the safety of higher ground. He took a steadying breath, and leaned forward to cautiously plant a hand on either side of her lush body.

No words could express his sorrow that he'd hurt her, so he gently began kissing the tears from her face instead. Coriander closed her eyes.

"Easy." The word slipped from her lips on a soft breath.

With each drop of salt that wet his lips Jude desperately prayed she would forgive him. It came as a surprise when he aimed to kiss the corner of her mouth and she turned into it with a small sound of contentment. He kissed the left corner, and before he could kiss the right, Coriander sighed and turned her face just enough that his mouth landed squarely on hers. He paused, his face only a breath over her. Jude's brow wrinkled.

Carefully, she reached a hand up to cup his face, using her thumb to massage the furrow in-between his eyes. "Just kiss me, Jude," she whispered as she pulled his mouth down to hers again.

Each slide of her mouth against his pulled him in deeper. There was nothing outside Coriander's mouth, the sensation of her silken body beneath his. As the hand he'd been using to steady himself slipped just enough to brush the side of her breast, she moaned into his mouth and leaned into his hand.

Jude broke their kiss and locked eyes with her. "I need you. I need to taste you. It's been so long."

She smiled, a shy, little curve of lips, and moved just long enough to position her head on a pillow. She lay before him like a feast, blessed and bountiful. And he was starving. It had been too long. Jude groaned, bending down to capture her mouth one last time, before trailing down her neck to the hollow of her throat. As careful as he could, he nipped the delicate flesh, darting his tongue out to savor the taste that was hers alone. It had been so long since he'd hungered for another that he fought the building urgency threatening to drain away all reason. Slowly, Jude forged a path of kisses and nips to her creamy breasts.

He was back in Heaven as he cupped one breast with his hand and let his tongue make a lazy circle around the nipple. He stared up the curving line of her body into her eyes. She was starting to breathe a little quicker, each flick of his tongue drawing short sounds from her parted lips. She whimpered and bit her bottom lip when his lips settled on her nipple and sucked. In the moonlight, the light sheen of sweat forming on her skin glimmered like liquid diamonds, and Jude planned on lapping up every one. As he alternated between sucking and gentle nibbling, he idly stroked the other nipple with his thumb.

Her next breath was ragged, and she shuddered as she arched her breasts into his hands, an invitation to touch more. He didn't have to be asked twice. His hand slid down her body, teasing over the mound of her sex, and the wild buck she made into his hand made him smile. He pressed down, feeling the slick wetness on his palm, and let his tongue travel down her abdomen to her belly button.

Coriander's head fell back with a guttural moan as he slipped one finger inside, teasing her. She gasped as his head descended lower, and his hand pulled away to brush the underside of her thigh and push. She was open before him, glistening and pink, ripe for plunder. It took every bit of resolve he had left to keep from shoving his face against her and devouring her on the spot.

Instead, he let the moist heat of breath ghost over her flesh. She whimpered with a wanton roll of her hips, bringing herself closer to his face. His tongue flicked out to trace the delicate folds and she cried out with abandon, reaching down to thread her hands in his hair. She pulled him close and he snarled with satisfaction as he dove into her.

Jude let his lips and tongue lave over her, licking and sucking, always careful to avoid the tiny nub begging for his attention. She writhed beneath his mouth, those fingers digging into his scalp to hold him in place. He took his time, his tongue piercing every fold, his lips kissing every inch of swollen, succulent flesh. Coriander's breath came in ragged, breathy gasps, her body struggling to remain still under his ministrations.

But he continued the seductive assault, taking both his hands and pressing back on her thighs. She almost came off the bed when the tip of his tongue poked at the turgid nub of her clit, screaming his name in a hoarse, throaty rasp. That one word lit the final fuse on his need, and he placed his mouth over the throbbing bud and sucked hard. Coriander screamed again, her body convulsing in soft tremors with her orgasm.

He licked her through the aftershocks, savoring the taste of her on his tongue, delighting at how beautifully she came apart. Jude kissed his way back up her body, grinning as her arms and legs wound around him in bliss, her mouth pressing to his flesh as he neared.

Jude's body vibrated with tension, wound tight with restraint. There was no pain. He marveled at that, but something still twisted beneath his flesh. He needed the release, needed to shake off the final vestiges of despair that burned in the shadowy corners of his soul. It was easy before to quiet the beast. It wanted pain and blood, it wanted the deep cuts and shallow breaths. And he had delivered. Now it had been banished with the gift of her touch, but what it left behind lingered on him like a film, clinging to his skin.

The urge to be inside her was overwhelming, and with every hitch in her breath and touch of her fingers, it was getting harder and harder to remember to go slow. He snorted out a rough breath as the pads of her fingers brushed across his length, cupping him gently. Coriander's lips found the underside of his jaw, and she nipped his skin with teasing bites as her thighs fell open in invitation.

"Please," she whispered, voice husky with desire.

He lowered his head. "I don't want to hurt you," he murmured against her shoulder.

"Please."

"Cori—I can't…I mean—"

Her finger pressed to his lips, shushing him. Eyes bright with passion sparkled back at him as she smiled, and the center of his chest swelled until he thought it would burst. She was so beautiful, so open. If he hurt her again, it would kill him. She wriggled her lower half, creating sparks of friction between their bodies. He groaned, eliciting another blinding smile.

"Trust me," she said, running her hands up his arms. "I'll let you know if it's too much."

His answer was to swoop down and capture her mouth in a fierce kiss. Remembering where it had been moments earlier, he tried to pull back, but she refused to let him, clutching him and moaning into his mouth. The low sound danced down his spine and pooled in his groin, making him harder. She made the most wonderful noises.

It was easy to shift his body to align with hers, centering himself at her entrance. He could feel the heat and wetness on the tip of his cock, and his hands slid down to tighten on her hips as he inched his way inside. His fingers curled into her flesh and she gasped. Jude stilled, panic crawling over him.

"It's okay. That was a happy noise."

He searched her face, looking for signs of distress, but found none. Her hands moved to wrap around his wrists as her hips arched upward.

"Keep going," she whined. "Happy noise."

The snorted half-laugh came unbidden at her pluck, and he shifted his hips a fraction, sliding further. She panted beneath him, urging him to move with little rolls of her body, squeezing her thighs to pull him in closer. When he could go no further, his head fell back on a strained groan.

Coriander was blistering heat and raging fires. Her body was primed for him, waiting for his touch. He thrust into her, the sensation washing over him in waves, and each snap of his hips had him driving harder and harder into her tightness. Jude growled as a haze filtered over his vision, blurring everything but the pounding need coiling at the base of his spine. His teeth ached under the force of it, each stroke pulling him inexorably closer to the edge.

She cried out, high and breathy, and he grabbed at her thigh to pull her leg around him. Coriander followed his lead with the other leg, wrapping herself around him. He could feel the dig of her heels in his back and her hands tightened around his wrists. He gripped harder, anchoring himself on her slight frame, knowing she would bear bruises tomorrow. The need was there, spiraling in the center of his chest, snaking out across his body in feverish tendrils of desire. There was no stopping it, nothing that could keep him from holding back.

Jude's head bent low to whisper in her ear, garbled words and half-phrases, choking back the well of sentiment he could neither discern nor express. The tattoo on his back blazed, his golden wings burning down to the bone, as if they would suddenly break free. He thrust, over and over again, until finally Coriander arched on a broken cry, shuddering out her release as she clung to him.

The sound of her voice pushed him over, and he rocked against her again before the coil of tension within him burst, his orgasm ripping through his body. Golden light shimmered behind his eyelids and his head fell back on a strangled groan. No pain. No hurt. Just light. Just Coriander.

She was so peaceful when she slept. It was hard for Jude to reconcile the wanton little thing she'd become last night with the slack-limbed beauty by his side. His hand itched to reach out and brush a stray lock of hair from her forehead, but he was afraid to wake her.

A terrible awkwardness settled into his bones as he eased onto his back, careful not to disturb her. What was this? Lucius would say it had been coming for months now, and he would be pleased that this dance between them had finally come full circle. But to what end? Was there an end? Somehow he knew when he left the bed and the sheets cooled, everything on the other side of the door would still remain. There would still be pain. There would still be an emptiness.

Even though what went on last night filled a void in his soul he never thought could be filled, there was still something missing. How in the world do you tell the woman you love that everything she is isn't enough to fix what's broken inside you?

Simple. You don't.

Jude eased out of the bed and dressed in silence, slipping out of the room. He cast one last, longing glance at Coriander and shut the door. Two steps down the hallway, the tattoo on his back burned with remembered fire. He gritted his teeth as his footsteps took him out of the house and into the gardens. It wasn't until moonlight blanketed him that he realized the burning was gone, and something else had taken its place. The pain in his soul was back.

The knowledge hit him in a rush, sending him staggering off the path into the yard as the pain became tangible. He gasped, his lungs pulling oxygen from the air with a white-knuckled yank. Everything burned, inside and out. There was no part of him untouched. It snaked down his arms in coils of white-hot heat, as if it would wrap around the corded muscle and cut straight to the bone. Jude stumbled as fire shot up from his toes, searing like a lightning strike, rendering his legs useless. He pitched to one side, grasping at the trunk of a giant oak tree for support. He registered the slickness of blood on his fingertips where they dug into the rough bark by scent alone.

The pain had no point of origin or precise point of entry, it merely was. His body flattened against the tree, pressing to crumple at the base of the trunk in an ungainly heap. The canopy of branches blocked out the slivers of moonlight, coating him in darkness. Jude's head lolled back as he fought to regain focus. His brain clamored to make sense of it all, to process and deal with it, but it swirled through him like a vortex, ripping the void wider. Everything rolled over him like fire in the desert, sweeping and devastating.

Memory warred with clarity in his mind's eye, and the gardens before him rippled and disappeared, leaving behind vast dunes of sand. They undulated across the desert, peaks and valleys, until the city came into view. The scent of sand and blood knocked him in the gut, the smell so powerful his throat clogged with the urge to gag.

The angels rampaged. They charged forth against the will of God, brazen in their disobedience, righteous in their fury. Golden wings spread out into the harsh rays of the sun, a shining, glorious wall of destruction. The blade in his hand shimmered, still golden underneath the stain of blood as he made his way through the city, bodies falling in his wake. The injured writhed in the streets and he stepped past, leaving the finishing blows to Mordecai and Elijah. Justice and Mercy. They would put it right. He was Vengeance. And he was here to deliver.

His sword arm ached with the force of each blow, each strike calculated to inflict as much pain as possible. He continued, hacking and slicing in his terrible rage, leaving no part of the city unturned, sparing neither age nor gender. Neither the innocent nor the guilty.

Dying fingers clutched at him as he passed, and he shrugged them off, swinging his sword with a terrifying grace. Blood flowed in the streets like a river, and he waded through it without a second thought. His heart swelled with pride at the crimson flood and the anguish in the air. It coated his tongue like honey, sweet and decadent, and he gave in to the feeling of pleasure. This was his purpose-- pain and death. This was his moment, his glory. This was what sustained him. Fulfilled him. Nothing else. Nothing. There was no room for anything but pain. It blossomed out from his chest and swallowed him whole. The sword clattered to the ground and he sank to his knees with open arms in supplication and let the pain take him.

"No!" Jude shouted, jerking up from the tree with a start. His breathing came in short, ragged wheezes,and he snorted twice to get himself under control. He closed his eyes at this past version of himself, wanting to deny the memory to his last breath. But there was no mistaking his vengeance. Or his sin. A soft breeze blew through, shaking the branches of the oak tree with a light rustle. He thought of Coriander, asleep and so beautiful, and began to cry.

"For whom do you weep, angel? Have I not given you respite enough for your pain?"

Jude's breath caught in his throat. *It couldn't be. Not now. Not after—*

"After you found a moment's peace within her arms?" The Voice said. "You knew your purpose long ago. Perhaps this is hers."

His heart hammered against his ribcage as his eyes searched the darkness. Nothing. The dried blood on his fingers was gritty as he swiped at the moisture on his cheeks. He couldn't dare to speak. Could he?

"You once found solace in Me, Jude." The Voice entreated.

"I—I tried, but You were gone," Jude stammered. His voice broke on a choked whisper. "Gone."

"Never too far. I have always watched over you. As I watch over all My children."

A gentle touch on his heart washed over him. A sensation he thought long dead. He closed his eyes, his heart heavy with regret and sorrow. Jude reached for anger and rage, emotions comfortable in their familiarity.

"Your anger is My tool. Your rage is My voice. And even when you thought Me gone, I nurtured those feelings within you. You will need them for the coming days."

His head thrashed from side to side as sudden, hot tears streamed down his face. "I should be angry," Jude snapped. "By all rights, I should be so fucking angry!" he shouted, kicking at the grass in front of him. His head shot up to the darkness, the tendons in his neck straining as he yelled, *"I am angry!"*

"Be still," The Voice said. "You may have your ire. It is in your nature. When I created you, I blessed you with all the things you would need to serve Me. Every breath you draw has purpose. Every emotion you feel has purpose. Every wound you deliver has purpose."

Jude sagged back against the tree, and pressed the heels of his palms over his eyes to stem the flow of tears as he whispered, "Then why I do I feel so lost?"

"You bear great responsibility on shoulders that already burn. There is still much to do before your path is clear. Everything you need has been laid before you. Avail yourself of My blessings and fulfill your redemption." Jude felt a rumble in his chest as the pain eased from searing to a dull ache. "You will be tested. You may succeed, and you may fail. Remember, angel, all ways in the end return to Me."

"How will I know what is right? I don't think I've made a good decision in the last thousand years." Jude blew out a breath as another breeze rippled through the tree. "How can I know which way to go? There is nothing for me but darkness."

The Voice was gentle and calming. "She has found you. And she will light your way. Trust in her as you once trusted in Me. Protect the light. Drive out the dark."

Jude closed his eyes and drew his knees up to his chest. This felt too easy. It couldn't be this simple. He couldn't sit back and let go of the anger, opening himself like that. His wounds were too deep, too ragged. Still as fresh as the day he fell. And now he was supposed to trust. He'd done that before, and look what happened.

"You were right to follow him," The Voice confirmed. "His choice was poor, but his heart was genuine. Loyalty to Lucius is loyalty to Me."

"I have always been loyal to Lucius," he said through gritted teeth. "Even when it was the wrong decision. I will always be loyal to Lucius." He shook his head. "I don't know about anyone else."

"Faith, My child. I am with you. Always."

The slight breeze was gone, leaving the stillness of the night. He was gone.

The ache in his heart spread out through his body, leaving a bitter aftertaste on his tongue. He licked dry lips and unfurled himself from the base of the tree into a stand, bracing one hand on the trunk for support. His body felt heavy, as if the weight of his soul rested on his shoulders. He waited for the joy at the Almighty's presence to surface. Joy he had been waiting for over lifetimes. Joy he was certain would come. Joy he *needed* to come. There was a measure of relief, of that there was no doubt, but as for anything more, well, that remained to be seen. He was told to have faith.

Faith. Jude snorted and shook his head. No, he needed more than tender mercies. What was one cryptic conversation in thousands of years? One tap on the shoulder after lifetimes of begging for acknowledgement. He was supposed to be happy with that? No. Not going to happen.

Jude followed the path back to the house and felt the air ripple around him as he moved. As he shed his clothes and slipped back into bed with a sleeping Coriander, he realized his moonlight confessional made one thing clear. He was still Vengeance. And he would never be appeased.

CHAPTER SIX

Ashtiru's laughter was almost as brilliant as the sky the next morning. Princess paddled around the swimming pool with her as Alex paced alongside. Jude watched it all through half-lidded eyes and groaned inwardly. She had coaxed him to come outside, that little spark of Coriander had burst into the bedroom and announced she was going swimming. Body-wide, his muscles ached, still a screaming piece of evidence of what had happened last night. Ash giggled, then gave a watery cough as Alex passed beneath the shade of a tree. Jude's eyes widened as the head of a jackal stared at him for moment before he blinked and Alex was squinting at him.

"You okay?" Jude asked. Alex grunted before he turned and grinned, a flash of white, at Ashtiru. That was when Coriander came outside in the white bikini. The spandex left little to the imagination. Jude knew Alex was staring at her as hard as he was. Beyond the general urge to bitch-slap him into say, next week, Jude's brain had shut down and his dick had officially taken over. Against her pale skin, bruises flashed on the curve of her hips. She bent to scoop up Ashtiru and spin her around. Those bruises were his trophies. Alex's head snapped up as Jude reddened. It was time to cool off. So Jude did the only thing natural that would quickly cool him and hide his obvious erection. Jude rolled off the lounge chair and took a running dive into the pool. The water was colder than he expected.

He tried to get his feet underneath himself, but instead opened his eyes as he sank toward the bottom, his lungs burning for air. His mouth opened to scream, water pouring in as the air left. Spots of black flashed in front of his eyes. The last thing Jude felt was the touch of cool slate beneath his body. His mind kept up the struggle to live, to find air.

He had almost forgotten that sound. It was bliss to his body, which burned. It was the sound of home, of Heaven. Warm, soft lips pressed against his and Jude reached with a hand, locked it into a tangle of silky, warm curls as he deepened the kiss. No pain, no fear greeted him in that kiss. However, a sharp pain erupted in his ribcage.

Jude rolled onto his side, water spilling from his lungs as he heard Khemrhy's voice snap, "You idiot! Why don't you pigeons learn? You can't swim. What possessed you to do that?"

Jude became aware of Khemrhy, soaking wet, dripping in a white sari next to him. He choked and struggled for breath. Khemrhy made an exasperated noise and kicked him in the abdomen. Water whooshed out of him and Jude inhaled deeply. He could hear the little girl crying. Fuck. Coriander was crying too. Double fuck. From his position on the ground, Khemrhy turned to Coriander and in a burst of steam was completely dry. She gently cradled Coriander's head on her shoulder and made soothing noises. "It's alright, my little girl. He'll live. Let Ashtiru see so she'll calm down."

Coriander set down the sobbing little girl and urged her toward the big angel. Jude sat up and tensed as he stared into those smoky green eyes. She sobbed, then sniffled, "Are you okay, Mr. Jude?" He nodded, afraid to scare the toddler away. Khemrhy might kill him or throw him back into the pool. Ashtiru reached out with a tiny brown hand and patted his cheek. The burn was subtle and developed into a dull ache in his bones. Ashtiru smiled a huge fox grin full of rainbows and sunshine. "He's okay, Mommy! You want to borrow my floaties, Mr. Jude? I have some pink ones you can use."

Jude's eyes bugged out as he spluttered, "No-no thanks, kiddo. I think I'll stay in the shallow end of the pool from now on." She kissed his cheek and ran back over to Khemrhy who picked her up to cradle her close. Her golden eyes flashed as Ashtiru said, "Grammy, will you come swimming with me and Princess?"

"Of course, my sweetling. Grammy will come after she's had a chance to change and deliver Mr. Winston's peony seeds to him." The girl clapped and Khemrhy set her down. She looked at Jude with a mild distaste. "Let's get you inside. Alex, come fetch him off his tail feathers and get him inside to fluff back out. Idiot." With that, her sandalled feet strode past him to the back doors. *Khemrhy was Coriander's mother.* Lucius would need to know that, amongst other things about the ex-goddess.

Lucius flinched as the door was flung wide. Instinctively, his wings flared, knocking into a display of pottery as Jude's voice bellowed, "Khemrhy's Coriander's mother, and I kissed her!"

The big angel's heavy, raspy breathing was punctuated by the clinking of pottery shards on the tile floor.

Lucius gaped and spluttered at Jude, "Khemrhy what?"

Jude was a wide-eyes dripping mess. His arms twitched and he took a watery breath to repeat himself. "She's her fucking mother! And if Cori is Seph's sister-"

Lucius held up a hand. "Why are you wet?"

As Jude started to answer, a gleaming perfection in while sailed in through the doorway. Lucius could feel heat rise in his cheeks as Khemrhy padded by in a white bikini that left little to the imagination, her cover-up draped artfully over one arm. Her curves were on display in a bright, mouth-watering scrap of spandex. Jude's head turned and caught a glimpse as she smiled, her full lips in a merlot up-turn as she hugged Persephone.

"Momma! What a surprise! What are you doing here?" Persephone cried.

Lucius' jaw snapped shut with a click. *Momma, meaning 'mother'.* His eyes went wide as Jude's as Khemrhry spoke soft and low to her daughter and left the room.

Coriander dropped the pile of towels, finding it oddly difficult to close her mouth. He was facing away from her, the black of his tattoo wings rippling across well-defined back muscles as he bent to set down the sack of food she had handed him. Domniel looked like some sort of Persian sex idol wearing nothing but black pants, with a crimson sash for a belt. It made Coriander wonder if he even realized, that left to his own devices, his living preferences were very similar to her mother's.

Her attention snapped back to the present as he quietly said, "Could you help me with something since you're here?" His voice was a little deeper, rougher as though he wasn't using it enough.

I can think of a few things to help you with. Where would you like me to start to licking? she thought, then blushed as Jude's face popped into her mind. Persephone was right. Dominick just made a girl think very dirty thoughts. She almost didn't recognize her own voice as she said, "What do you need?" *Oh shit! Am I flirting?*

Domniel slowly turned to face her, his voice like liquid sex, "I don't think it would be wise for you to offer up anything about needs, Coriander. Jude would probably kill me. Or at least make a valiant attempt."

Her temper flared. "Yeah, well, Mr. Broody is having issues of his own. He's back at the main house having fits because he made out with my mother when she was trying to give him CPR. Keeps freaking out because he," she made air quotes, "'kissed Khemrhy'. Like it's some big damn deal." The room got hotter, and Cori looked up to find Domniel standing directly in front of her, holding out his hand.

"Why don't you take me up to the house and I'll talk to him about it? I'll get him to chill out."

"My pottery!" Coriander shrieked. Jude whirled in the direction of the door and saw her standing there with a face full of ire. Domniel stood behind her, holding tightly to her tiny hand.

"I didn't break it. Lucius did it," he stammered as she let go of Domniel and bent to the shards on the floor with a noise of irritation. Domniel carefully scooted around her and shuffled over to him, frowning.

"What's got you in such a twist?" he asked. Domniel was silent, his chest heaving. Jude sighed out the breath he'd been holding. Then everything sped up.

Snarling, Domniel was fast as he grabbed Jude's throat in his hot, tight hand and shoved him against the wall. Jude struggled for air as fire lit every nerve. Domniel's blind eyes burned a brilliant blue as his face narrowed the space between them. He bared his teeth as Jude tried to pry the hand from his throat.

"Let's get something straight. Whatever you felt when you laid your mouth on Khemhry's? You swallow that shit. I will personally," his voice deepened to a low growl, "fuck you up if you ever lay a hand on her again. You got it...brother?"

Jude nodded as spots danced into front of his eyes. Air hit his lungs with nuclear force as Domniel let him go and he sank to his knees next to Coriander. He watched Domniel leave with caution. This day was getting worse and worse. All he wanted to do was curl up on the bed with Coriander and take a nap.

It was easy enough to sneak onto the property unnoticed. The noise from the back of the house suggested all the occupants were in the pool area. The Dealer placed his hand on the large brass doorknob, and let a trickle of power flow through his fingers. The knob turned with a gentle click. He stepped inside, careful to make no sound as his brain filtered through the images he had collected. His feet moved of their own accord, as if he had prior knowledge of the layout of the house, his steps taking him directly to the archeologist's office.

His eyes sought out the glass case from his memories, and sure enough, it sat in its spot on the wall-to-wall cabinetry behind the large desk. As he neared, he realized what was wrong. He couldn't feel the essence of the amulet. The case was empty.

Lips curling into a nasty sneer, he let his power fan out, searching for a trace of the object. Nothing. It was gone. He wouldn't have the chance to tear the place apart to find it. A vile mix of anger and arrogance fueled his blood as he decided on a course of action. A glint of gold in the corner caught his eye, and he turned to come face to face with the golden death mask.

A plan clicked into place as he stared into the lapis eyes of the dead pharaoh. The Dealer's lips softened, the harshness receding as he took in a deep breath.

Akhenaten. Of course. The images flipped through his mind once again. *The progeny. Perfect.*

He slipped back to the front door and out of the house, and made his way to the edge of the property. Night would fall soon, and he would strike. He still had time—granted, not much-- but if everything went as smoothly as he thought it would, then he would be back to stand in front of the Dark Lord and claim his reward. How much trouble could one little girl be?

The bushes only rustled a moment. Ashtiru held her breath as she peered between the leaves at the pair of worn, brown loafers that tried to sneak up on her. Princess wiggled, making the bush rustle again. Ashtiru squinted in the early morning light, and pulled at the hook on Princess's collar. This stranger, who smelled like the matches she'd used to light Mommy's carpet on fire, didn't need to know that Princess wasn't a normal badger. All she'd wanted to see was her Uncle Winston's morning glories opening, so she'd gone outside to watch them. Then the stranger had shown up.

Ashtiru squatted between two of the purple flowers, trying to pick the petals as they opened, when the light became blackened by the outline of a tall man. The "bad feeling" crept over her skin, so she sneaked away like Mommy had taught her to, careful to stay silent. Quietly, Princess waddled out of the bush, and Ashtiru let her breath out as the bad man's feet turned and walked away. Suddenly, Ashtiru wanted her mommy bad enough that she bit her lip and stifled a sob with her hand. Her eyes widened as she saw the bad man stop and sniff like he was smelling her. Princess ceased in her bumbling and growled at him. Silently, he bent to the badger and inhaled. His gray head sniffed really deep as Ashtiru struggled to hold her breath. Finally, Princess bared her teeth and the stranger's head jerked toward her. A giant, clawed, burning hand slammed onto Princess, crushing her underneath it.

Ashtiru screamed and stood up as the bad man killed Princess. A set of angry, glowing orange eyes that looked like melting pumpkins jerked to stare at her.

"Got you!" he rasped. Ashtiru screamed again and ran. Bushes and trees flew by as she ran on tiny legs, never noticing the fallen log.

She tripped and landed hard on her knees, scraping the tender skin off as she wailed. Hands as hard and cold as ice grabbed her and pulled her to the matchstick man.

As the sun rose, Ashtiru's cries folded into the setting shadows of night.

Coriander frowned. She looked around the Cheerio-scattered kitchen, fighting the bird about to push from her chest. "Ashtiru? Baby? Come out now. You win." She raised her voice as her eyes kept landing on the back door.

It was cracked open, and tiny smudges formed a trail from the door to the badger's food dish. Coriander's heart rate began a staccato beat as hard as her sister's crazy, horny, Irish drummers could bang out. She opened the door, expecting her child to be on the other side.

The empty walkway showed her nothing.

Coriander never understood anything as she turned and walked back to the entry to the rest of her house, eyes wide and teary. She didn't think as she leaned on the doorframe, pressing a white-knuckled fist to her chest and screamed, "Alex! *Alex!*"

A door banged from somewhere upstairs, followed by the quick slaps of Alex's feet on the stairs. He skidded to a stop inches from her, completely naked, dripping wet, and breathing hard.

"What the hell, Cori?" he gasped between breaths. "I was in the shower-"

"Ash," she panted, "Ashtiru's..." Coriander's body began to shake as angels piled into the kitchen. Somewhere in the next few minutes, amidst Coriander's sobbing in Greek and hysterical crying, queries delivered in soft voices and Alex managing to get on a pair of sweatpants snatched from an errant laundry basket, no one could get a word out of Coriander.

Lucius rubbed his scruffy chin and said to Jude, "I can't get anything out of her that doesn't involve Cheerios, a badger, and something about a bird."

As Jude opened his mouth to respond, a deep, gravelly voice said, "She's missing. She snuck off this morning." Every head turned to see Domniel towering in the doorway.

No one was quick enough to stop Coriander as she flung herself at Domniel, screaming, "Where? Where is my baby?"

Domniel was almost terrifying, his eyes blocked by a heavy swath of black fabric, blindfolding them. His lip curled, "What kind of a fucking mother are you that you don't know where your little waste of sperm is?"

Every woman in the kitchen gasped as if he'd slapped Coriander. The redhead's eyes narrowed as she hauled back her arm, palm open wide.

A steely, cool hand locked around her wrist and Lucius croaked out, "Don't."

He looked to Domniel and asked, "Did you hear her?" The blind angel nodded. "When?" Lucius asked again as he steered Coriander into Jude's grasp.

Domniel's head tilted in thought, his dark hair tumbling over his forehead to cover the front of his face. "About sunrise. So, maybe an hour ago. Little shit makes a lot of noise…then again, so does that fucking badger."

Lucius nodded. "Thank you, Domniel. I'd say go and get some rest, but we have to find her. Did she go north or south?"

Domniel's lips and jaw hardened as he said, "South. She went south." He straightened to a stiff stand and waited before saying, "I heard screaming, Lucius."

Everything exploded as Coriander belted past Domniel and out the door, screaming her daughter's name. Persephone and Teraslynn raced after her.

Domniel turned and growled, "Happy hunting," as he left. The four angels stared at each other, Alex catching their glances.

"How many acres to the south?" Mordecai asked.

"About fifty or sixty, I think," Alex answered as he stepped in front of the gathered angels and undid the drawstring on his sweats. "Most of the acreage is wooded, so you'll need a good nose to find any trace of Ashtiru." The little girl's name was rich and resonant on his tongue, with a definite Middle Eastern curl on his accent. His sweatpants hit the floor as he got naked and looked at four pairs of shocked, raised eyebrows. Alex's face set into a hard mask as he glared at them. "No questions." In a bright flash of blue light, Alex was gone.

The sandy colored dog, its big ears pointed sharp and its snout narrow, was big. It stared at each angel with deep, cinnamon-colored eyes before looking to the back door. It whined as it trotted to the kitchen table and nosed at the crinkled box of Cheerios.

"You want a treat, boy?" Mordecai snickered as he reached for the box. A growl was punctuated with quick huffs of its muzzle. The deaf angel set the box on the floor and stepped back as the dog rammed his snout in the box. The dog snuffled in the box for a moment, and then shook the box off. The hackles on its back raised as it released an unearthly growl, followed by a blood-curdling howl. It took off like a shot out the open door, leaving the angels to gape at one another in befuddled silence.

"Well," Lucius said on a low breath, "I sure as fuck wasn't expecting that."

Jude stared at the mess of Cheerios and Alex's discarded sweatpants on the floor. "You and me both, boss. You and me both."

Jude wiped the sweat from his brow again as he thought about the last six hours. They had been tromping through the woods, calling Ashtiru's name. The dog, which he had begrudgingly reconciled as Alex in his mind, had turned out to be quite useful to the search party. Luckily, they were about fourteen people strong on the ground, and Lucius had taken to the air.

He pushed another branch out of his way, and flinched as a rabbit bolted for the safety of its warren. Coriander's crazy, Irish sister had turned out to be useful as well. Her band members were equally noisy, like a giant murder of crows as they entered the search, each with a drum in tow. They had fanned out after a moment and disappeared.

Jude's head snapped as a booming bass of a drum came from his left. It was followed by a large amount of whistling and shouting in what sounded like Gaelic.

Bells jingled rhythmically on his right and Teraslynn burst from between two trees, Coriander right behind her. Coriander locked wide eyes with his as she gasped, "Seamus found something." Jude followed them.

The badger, Princess, lay in a mashed heap beneath morning glory vines. The froth on her jaw was bloody, her eyes closed in pain. Jude hugged Coriander close as Seamus explained how he found her, while running his hand around the rim of his doumbek in nervousness. Seamus, like most of the musicians, didn't speak English, instead using a combination of Arabic and Gaelic. Jude caught tail ends of the Arabic, but the rest might as well been the Greek Coriander and Alex preferred.

Coriander and Teraslynn understood it all. There was some soft crying before they left the badger in peace to look for Ashtiru again.

It came upon Jude unexpectedly. The shoe, a little white sandal, peeked out from underneath the edge of a fallen log. Jude kicked the rest of it aside and stared at the smashed piece of delicate footwear, the growing tightness in his chest threatening to cut off his air. He closed his eyes, the brush rustling as Alex sniffed around. Brimstone filled his nose and he choked as he heard Alex's plaintive whine. The dog nudged his leg with a wet snuffle, and then leaned down to nose at the shoe. His body stiffened in response to the demon scent. And from the stench permeating this section of the woods, it was powerful. His wings burned as rage filled him, and it took him a moment to realize that Alex wasn't the one growling.

Jude put two fingers to his lips and whistled for the others.

Every moment for Coriander was an eternity. Finally, it was over. She cradled the shoe, her hand shaking and her teeth sinking into the flesh of her bottom lip hard enough to break skin. Jude. Jude had found it, the last vestige of her precious baby. She could remember how much Ashtiru loved her white sandals. The sandal twitched in her hand, hard enough to drop. Coriander gasped and fumbled to hold it tighter. She knew the moment she opened her mouth she would start screaming and probably never stop, so she held it tighter and cradled it close to her face. Coriander breathed deep and sulfur filled her nose. A million terrifying memories screamed in her mind at the smell: her mother, her father, and the demon. Coriander opened her mouth and screamed.

CHAPTER SEVEN

By the time they realized little Ash was well and truly gone, Coriander had worked herself into a strop of biblical proportions. Jude and the other angels stood back and watched, helpless in bewildered confusion as the tiny redhead exploded in a tirade of righteous fear. She screamed at the top of her lungs while Alex and Winston trailed after her, frantically trying to get her to calm down.

The point of convergence seemed to be Coriander's office, where they all filed in to see her crying out in hysterics over a crumpled note in her hand. She sobbed and flailed in a wild mass of flying limbs, making it impossible for anyone to get close. It wasn't until Teraslynn stepped up and delivered a whistling, open-handed slap to her sister's cheek that things began to settle.

The crack of Teraslynn's hand against Coriander's cheek echoed through the room, and snapped her head back. Jude held his breath as Coriander's green eyes focused from glassy terror to outright anger.

"Jaysus', Cori! Would you shut it?" Teraslynn yelled. "We won't get fecking' anywhere with you ranting like a thrice-damned banshee!"

The murderous glare in Coriander's eyes was trained on her sister for a moment before her face drooped and she stumbled into Teraslynn's outstretched arms. The willowy blonde held Coriander gently, murmuring soft Gaelic into her ear. She plucked the crumpled note from Coriander's grasp and handed it off to Alex as Persephone sidled in, wrapping her arms around the sisters.

Jude looked sharply at Alex. "What does it say?"

Alex unfolded the paper as his eyes scanned over it, shadows crossing his features. "We have a week. Bring him the amulet and he returns Ash. If not, he'll kill her."

Coriander screamed again and Jude felt the air squeeze from his lungs. "What amulet?" he asked.

The redhead choked out, "The same one you tried to take from me the first time we met. It's the only one I have. I don't even know what it does."

Jude's voice cut like steel. "It's going to get your daughter back."

Lucius' voice was soft. "Where did it take her?"

"It?" Alex asked.

"Demon. Don't tell me you didn't smell the brimstone with that nose."

Alex's face went pale. "It's been a long time."

"So where is it?" Jude asked.

Alex shook his head. "Not sure." He handed the note over to Jude. "'One daughter sleeps while one daughter dies.' What the fuck does that mean?"

Coriander's head snapped up. "Daughter?" She scrabbled for the note, panicked eyes reading over it again. "The statue. *Meketaten*," she whispered. She ran to the glass case in the corner of the room. The note fell from her hands as she pressed them against the case with the death mask. "Akhenaten's daughter. He knows this piece. That's why he was here. He was supposed to deliver the statue." She turned back around, frightened eyes glassy with panic. "He's taken her to Egypt," she said with certainty. "To Meketaten's tomb."

Coriander was a dervish, rushing out the office to whirl around the living room in a panic, her tiny hands flailing in the air. "Cairo. We have to get to Cairo." She rounded on Alex. "Look," she said, grabbing at him, "we have to get in touch with the Egyptian authorities. Monitor traffic in and out. Maybe we can find her that way. Do you still have your contacts in Immigration? It'll be a rush," she panted, digging in her pockets for her cell phone, "but maybe we can get a charter and leave tonight. We'll need papers and maybe a team. I'll have to find the tomb. Avalon. I need Avalon. She knows the texts. She can help me find it." She was babbling now as she pushed at Alex. "Go on, go pack. Go!" She pushed harder, but the dark-haired man didn't move. Jude watched his face tighten.

"Cori," Alex said softly. "You know I can't. I'm sorry. We'll find another way."

"No!" she screeched. "You get on the phone! You get us a fucking flight! I won't let him take her like this! I can't-I won't...I-" She broke down, and Alex caught her before she hit the floor.

"It's okay, Cori. We'll find her. We'll get her back." Alex's eyes found Jude's over Coriander's hair, beseeching him.

Jude stepped forward, and Alex turned her gently into his arms. The rest of the room erupted in a frenzy of shouts as the enormity hit home. Coriander pushed out of his hold and into the mass of bodies, adding to the noise.

"Will everyone just calm the hell down?" Jude roared. The room silenced instantly. Lucius opened his mouth to step forward, but Jude shoved a hand in his face. "Not now, boss."

His leader pursed his lips and gave him a long look, then relaxed and remained silent. Jude felt a twinge of guilt at putting the kibosh on Lucius. He'd never overstepped before. He had never needed to, but this was Ash. And there was something about that little girl that tore open his heart. They had to find her.

"I can't go, Coriander." Alex's voice was soft, tinged with heartache, and he could see the effect the gentle tone had on her. Her shoulders slumped and a tiny sigh escaped her.

"Why can't you go?" Jude blurted, enraged that the other man could be so calm. "She's your daughter, for fuck's sake! If she were mine, I would tear this world apart to find her!"

"But she's not yours," Alex snapped. "And don't you presume to tell me how to handle this. She's my child, and it's killing me—" his voice broke in a harsh sob, "fucking killing me."

"I know, Alex," she said. "You have to stay." She shook her head and lifted her chin. "One of us needs to be here for Ash." She broke from him and pulled Alex into a hug, pressing a kiss to the top of his head as he buried it in her shoulder. "We'll find her. We'll bring her home."

Jude bristled and drew himself up, anger fuelling his words. "This isn't my place. If anyone should be going—"

"He can't!" Coriander barked, letting Alex go. "And that's the end of it. If you don't want to go with me, fine, I'll go on my own. But he stays."

Her words were firm, determination and fire shining in her eyes. She would go on her own, he had no doubt. She'd go, and knowing that stubborn streak, get herself killed. He thought about Lucius and the others, but had a feeling if the kidnapper knew they were all traipsing around after him, little Ash didn't stand a chance. He'd kill her.

Jude looked over at Alex, able to see the worry and the guilt stretched on his face. Maybe the dog had a good reason for not going to fetch his daughter. Maybe. But as the memory of Ashtiru's light laughter filtered into his ears, he couldn't imagine what it could be. Because if she was *his* kid, he'd give The Almighty the finger and fall all over again at the chance to save her.

He set his shoulders in a hard line and crossed his arms over his chest. "Fine. I'll go, if only to keep you from getting killed in the process."

Coriander let out a sorrowful whine and threw herself at him in a tight hug. Coolness slid over his skin, and he wrapped his arms around her. He met Alex's eyes over the top of her head, and the other man gave a sharp nod in return. Jude watched as Alex turned and left them alone in the room.

She shuffled in his grasp and pulled back. "Thank you," she whispered. "I know we can find her."

His lips pursed in a tight line, unable to manage a reply. Jude pulled her back to the circle of his arms and let her sag against him. It was going to be a long couple of days. And he fucking hated Egypt.

The mood was tense as evening slipped into moonlight. Emotions ran high as Alex watched the angels flock to Coriander and offer her words of comfort he knew were of no use. Nothing would comfort her until Ashtiru was safely home once again. Persephone was just as much of a wreck as her sister, and he watched her cling to Lucius in a quiet bundle of sobs. They rose from the couch, and the blonde woman gave Coriander one last hug before the angel ushered her up the stairs to retire for the evening.

The noisy one, Alex had only met her a handful of times, was reserved now, grasping Coriander's hand tightly in her own. She squeezed it before announcing she would spend the night with her bandmates in the caravan outside. He heard something about "strength in numbers" before she headed out the front door. The blind one had yet to make an appearance, and frankly, given the volatility of the situation, his absence was probably a good thing. The deaf one and the mute sat together on the opposite sofa, side by side, practically sharing a cushion. Their hands were intertwined as well. They projected an odd strength, tempered with gentleness, and he wondered about the closeness that came so easily to the pair. Their worry and concern was evident, a united front against the evil that had transpired.

Alex saw them share a look and an unspoken word, just a gesture of fingers, and then they rose as one. They smiled at him with sympathy and crossed to Coriander. She hugged each one in turn, and they were gone as well. It was then that he met Jude's eyes.

The big angel said nothing, and wrapped his arms around Coriander. It hurt, he had to admit, but the sting was mitigated over the blatant concern in the angel's face. Whatever was going on, he had genuine emotion for both Ashtiru and her mother. *Point to you, sir. That makes what I'm about to tell you so much easier.*

Coriander sniffed and wiped her face with the back of her hand. "It's late, and there's nothing we can do now. We can start fresh in the morning and make a game plan. I'll get Avalon here as quick as I can." She extricated herself from Jude's grasp and went to the stairs.

The words were out before he could call them back. "Jude, a word."

"Sure."

Coriander didn't bother to look down from her ascent. "Don't keep him too long, Alex."

"I won't." Alex gestured to the parlor at the other end of the living room. "Drink?"

Jude sighed and his shoulders sagged. "Make it a double."

Alex shut the door behind them and proceeded to pour two generous glasses of something from a crystal decanter. He sniffed one glass experimentally. Scotch. Single malt. Old. Perfect. Something told him this conversation would require top shelf booze. He handed a glass to Jude.

"I feel like we've been here before," the angel smirked.

Alex smiled as he sat down. "Yeah, let's not revisit that ending, shall we?"

"I have a problem with you not going," Jude said flatly.

"Good to see you're not wasting time with pleasantries," Alex shot back.

"I don't think we have time for the bullshit, do you? Your little girl is out there—"

Alex sat up and snapped, "I know that. But you need to know why I can't go."

"I don't fucking care. Whatever it is, sack up and get out there. Cori needs you." Jude sat down and gulped the contents of his glass. "I'm nobody's replacement."

Alex felt his face pinch and his cheeks flush with anger. "We're really going to go here, aren't we? I thought we settled this." He took a sip of the scotch, needing the burn to keep going. "And you couldn't replace me if you tried."

Jude paused for a moment and sighed. "You're right," he admitted. "The dick-swinging is getting old. Spill."

Alex placed his glass on the low table and sat back to rub a hand over his face. "If he had taken her anywhere else, I would be out there so fast it would make your head spin. It's Egypt. I can't return to Egypt."

The big angel's eyebrow quirked in amusement. "Piss off the government? Been banned from the country?" He leaned forward. "I didn't think something as little as that would keep a man like you grounded. Afraid of being arrested?"

Alex shook his head. "I'm afraid it's a little more dramatic than prison." He ran the words over in his head, unable to find a better way to express himself. "If I go back to Egypt, I will die."

Jude snorted. "Now who's being dramatic?"

He narrowed his eyes on the angel. "Do you remember the conversation we had? Pretty blue lights over my stylish mop of hair? Ring a bell?"

"What of it?"

"I'm going to say this slowly, so perhaps you'll understand me this time." Jude frowned at him, but he continued. "Anubis," Alex enunciated with a heavy drip of sarcasm. "Well, one of a long line, anyway. Let's just say that a very long time ago, the Anubis left Egypt with the caveat that should he ever return, death is pretty much guaranteed."

"You get that in writing? Or is this just shitty speculation?" Jude asked with a sardonic smile.

"Fuck you, it's the truth. The point is, I don't even remember the past lives I'm supposed to have led. I get flashes every now and then, but nothing that makes any real sense. The light show," he waved a finger over his head, "it's like a divine warning symbol to those in the know. Sort of a 'hey, don't lie to this guy, the blue jackal can tell'. Weighing of the heart, and all that. Been quite useful in my work." At Jude's snort of disbelief, he frowned. "For whatever reason, curse, destiny, fate, divine cruelty, whatever you want to call it, if I dig a toe in Egyptian sand, I will die there. So, let me ask you which one is a better choice. Both Cori and I going and taking the chance that neither one of us makes it home, or me staying here, making sure Ash has a parent to come home to?"

Jude said nothing, but the shadow that crossed his face told Alex the big angel was mulling it over.

"You know there's a good chance Cori won't make it back. It's a given that I won't. I can't risk going and then something happening to Coriander. Then where does that leave Ash? Down two parents instead of one. Do the math." He didn't know if trying to make the angel see things from his point of view would make any difference. He knew he certainly wasn't currying any favor, either. They'd at least managed a civil conversation long enough without resorting to violence and bloodshed. A small part of him lamented that fact, but then again, they had only started to drink. There was still time. And there was more than enough booze for the effort.

As if the big angel read his mind, Jude got up and poured himself another scotch, slamming it back without preamble. He wiped the back of his hand over his mouth and pointed at Alex. "I know what you're doing. This noble shit. Don't. Don't make me start to like you. I don't want to like you."

"I don't care if you like me, Jude, I just need you to keep her safe. Because this time, I can't. And it kills me." *More than you will ever know.*

Jude shook his head and let out a groan Alex knew well. Frustration. He waggled a finger in Alex's direction. "No, no. This is not what I do. I can't swoop in and save the day. There will be no heroics, no epic destruction, no feats of supernatural savioring." He jerked a thumb at his back. "These are just for show, buddy. They don't work. I played hero once and it was a mistake. I'm going to hang back and make sure she doesn't shoot her foot off. Or mine. That's it. We find Ash and bring her home."

"She believes in you." Once again, the words bled out of his mouth on a sting. "Coriander has faith in you." Alex paused and considered the big angel and his awkwardness at their impromptu confessions. "She's a smart woman. Maybe she's right."

He put down the glass and frowned back at Alex. "She's too mouthy for her own good. Never seen a woman who could talk so much and not say a damn thing."

"You love her," he blurted. Jude's eyes went wide and Alex had to smile. "You do." He leaned back, enjoying the look of abject terror that crossed the angel's face. "And it's freaking you out." He threw his head back and laughed. "God, this is rich. I was worried before, but this... oh, Christ—you really don't know what you're going to do with her, do you?"

"Shut up."

Alex stood and moved across the room to stand in front of Jude. The big angel's eyes flitted around him, and he knew he was taking in the light show. He pointed to his head. "Can't lie to me, remember?" Alex narrowed his eyes, knowing they would darken to slits. The image wasn't terrifying, but it managed to unnerve most people. Jude was no exception. "It's the weighing of your heart." His hand came up to poke Jude in the chest. The angel didn't flinch. "I can see right through you."

The shock had drained from the angel's eyes, replaced by a calm and calculating scrutiny. The big angel wasn't objecting to being read, per se; it was the truth being pointed out that he didn't like.

"And what do you think you see?" Jude's voice held an undercurrent of warning.

"I see your darkness." Alex let his eyes rove over the angel, watching as his Adam's apple bobbed with a hard swallow. Jude's nostrils flared and the fingers of one hand flexed, not quite curling into a fist. He was holding back, restraining himself. "I see your pain. And when you talk about her, I see golden light. Truth. Love." He stepped back to give Jude some room. "Whether or not you want to admit to me, it's true, and you know it. You love her. And Ash, in your own way."

"How does that make you feel?" There was a catch to Jude's voice. Guilt? Regret? It was hard to place. But the emotion was genuine. No reason not to reward honesty with honesty.

"I hate it," he said simply. "But I have no choice. Just make them happy."

"I'll try. That's all I can promise."

Alex's eyes danced over Jude again, soaking in the truth of the big angel's words. "Yeah, but that's enough for me."

The big angel downed the rest of his drink and set the glass down hard. Jude rose to his feet and headed for the doorway. "I sure as hell hope you mean that, because if you come at me again, it won't be Egypt you have to worry about." The angel didn't wait for a response and left, heavy footsteps echoing across the floor.

Alex flicked two fingers in a mock salute at the empty doorway. "Noted."

CHAPTER EIGHT

Jude wasn't surprised to see her small frame curled up on his bed when he entered the room. Her own bedroom, he surmised, would be filled with photos and other reminders of Ash. The guest room was neutral ground. Easy enough for her to escape to.

"Hey," he ventured, shutting the door softly.

Coriander sat up, her face pale and drawn. The sparkle was gone from her green eyes, leaving them flat and lifeless against the wan pallor of her skin. She wiped a shaky hand over her face and stood up, turning her back to him as she paced the room. Jude leaned back against the door, not wanting to crowd her.

Tension had her shoulders and spine stiff with worry, and she walked with a slight hitch, as if each of her steps were weighted. She moved in front of the dresser, trailing her fingers over the expanse of wood. They drifted among the few items he had left scattered about; a small stack of cash he'd folded for Domniel, a few coins, and some receipts. She didn't speak until her fingertips caught the edge of the small, obsidian blade. Her eyes darted up to the mirror and honed in on his reflection.

"This is mine," she said, her lips lifting at the edges. "Now who's the thief?"

He shrugged. "Comes with the territory, I suppose."

"I suppose."

"Who's Avalon?" he asked.

"The last of my sisters. The smart one. She's quiet. Bookish." Coriander's smile was wan. "She can help me get her back."

Jude pushed off from the door. "Cori—"

"How do you do it?" she asked, holding the little dagger in her palm for him to see.

"Do what?" He stopped short, but moved to the bed. The mattress gave a heavy squeak as he shifted.

"Deal with the pain." A twinkle appeared in her eyes, but it was wild and manic, as evidenced by the sudden flush to her cheeks. "Is that why I find you in the tub so often, bleeding your cares away? Does it hurt so bad that you have to—" her voice broke, "cut the pain out?"

Jude frowned and crossed the room in a flash, snatching the blade from her grasp. "Stop it," he chided. "Get a hold of yourself, Cori. You don't know what you're saying."

"Like hell!" she snapped, beating her fist against her chest. "It hurts, damn it! My baby's gone and it hurts!"

His hands wound around her and pulled her close. "I know it does, babe. I know." He pressed a soft kiss into the crown of her head. Coriander leaned into the caress, and rubbed her face against his chest as she shook with small tremors.

"Is this what it's like for you?" she whispered. "All the time? This burning? I can't—I don't…"

Jude eased them over to the bed, keeping her secure in the cradle of his arms. "You want to know what it's like?" She nodded and sniffled into his shirt. "It's worse," he sighed. "Whatever you're feeling—the pain, the ache. All of that, yeah, it's a thousand times worse. It's constant. And it's not just inside, either. I can feel it on my skin and in my bones, like it's alive, eating me. It doesn't stop. It...persists. It exists. Breathes my air and steals my soul. And I can't ever get rid of it. So, yeah, it's worse. Because I deserve it." He squeezed her tighter. "But this? This is nothing you can't handle. We'll find Ash. And this will go away."

Coriander whimpered and clutched at him. He buried his face in her hair, feeling his own tears rising to the surface. "How do you stand it?" she gasped. "How does it not drive you crazy?"

He reached out and covered the hand that held the dagger in his own. "The knife," he said quietly. "It's kind of like you said. Only there's nothing to cut out. Because it's me. I am the pain. And on the other side of that is pleasure. I can't have one without the other. Sometimes it's the only thing that keeps me sane. It's the one thing He left me." He smoothed a stray lock of hair off her face as she lifted her head and stared up at him.

"And now?"

The wildness vanished from her eyes, shining instead with a bright hope that took his breath away. He swallowed the lump in his throat and smiled, unable to stop it from spreading across his face like an oil spill. "Now there's you."

Her body curled into his and he gathered her closer, settling them both back against the headboard. Jude ran his hand down the softness of her arm and found her fingers. He let his hand play along the spaces in between before linking their fingers together, relishing the slide of her calloused palm against his.

"Talk to me." Her voice was muffled against his chest.

"About?"

She let out a slow breath as she shifted, turning her body to put them chest to chest. Her other hand lingered along the hem of his t-shirt for a few seconds, then moved underneath to lay flat on his stomach. She kept her hand still, just above the waistband of his jeans.

"Tell me what happened. Tell me how you fell."

Jude's gut clenched. "I don't think now is a good time-"

"It's as good a time as any," she interrupted. "And somehow I don't think there is a good opening for this story. So tell me now."

He sighed. She was right. There would never be an appropriate time to bring up the sins of the past. Might as well bite the bullet and tell her everything. If anything, she needed the distraction.

"There was a city. A long time ago. And we were there to observe. Just observe." He took a breath as the memory came back to him. "It was fine for a while, and we did as we were told. We watched."

"What happened?"

"Outsiders. They tore down the city walls and invaded. There was blood and death, and we watched." Jude shifted as his breathing hitched with the weight of the memory. "There was a siege, and the people didn't stand a chance. They were being slaughtered."

She shuddered against him. "That must have been terrible, having to see that and not being able to interfere."

He pressed a kiss to the top of her head. "Yeah. It was. But we kept back. Like we were told."

"So what changed?"

"I'm not sure." Jude's brow furrowed. "It was getting harder and harder to stay out of it. There were so many dying, Cori. Innocents. Children. And they were falling to the outside forces. Lucius was firm. We were to do nothing. Let it happen."

Coriander raised her head to look at him. Her eyes were wide with concern, and her lips parted on a soft rush of air. "But you didn't let it happen, did you? You saved them?" The hope in her voice was chilling, cutting him to the core. He saw her faith shining in her eyes, the belief in his station as angelic protector written across her face. Would that light die when he told her the truth? He bit his bottom lip as the words sat on the tip of his tongue, bitter and foul.

"No."

She gasped, the small sound piercing his heart. "What did you do?"

Jude took a deep breath and pressed her head down to his chest. He could say it was because he wanted to have her as close as possible, but the truth of it was he didn't want to see her eyes when he told her the truth.

"Lucius-," he started, "he grew restless. We all did." Jude closed his eyes and sniffed. "We watched for so long. It was so hard to believe that this was His plan for these people. To die like that. And then there was Lucifer-"

Coriander sat up. "Lucifer? You don't mean…" Her question trailed off as he nodded.

"Yeah. *The Morning Star*," he sneered. "By this time, the asshole had already made his choice. But he was in Lucius' ear, and things between all of us were strained. We were angry with him, sure, but at the time, we still thought of him as a brother." The term of endearment tasted like shit on his lips. "And he was so convincing, you know, right there, just whispering. In hindsight, it was so easy to see how he played Lucius. How he played all of us." Jude's lip curled in disgust. "Silver-tongued bastard. Part of me hopes he spends his days getting fucked six ways from Sunday with a brimstone cock the size of an elephant." He blew out a harsh breath. "Even that would be too good for him."

"What did he say? I mean, did you still trust him?"

"Yes." He shook his head. "No. It was complicated and painful. He had turned his back on all of us, we thought, and then there he was, saying all the right things to push all the right buttons, and before we knew it, Lucius had lost it and we followed him. Because we always followed Lucius. He twisted things, made us all doubt. I mean, what kind of God would allow for the suffering that we witnessed? Lucius believed the crap that Lucifer was spitting out. We ached for these people, and it made sense that we could do something about it. It made sense that we could put a stop to it."

The flat of her hand pressed harder on his skin, rubbing in small, soothing circles. "How did you stop it? Did you stop it?"

He swallowed, and felt the emptiness pool in his gut. "We did more than stop it. We killed them all. The innocent and the outsiders."

Jude felt her stiffen and clutch him tighter as a small cry escaped her lips. "Why?" she whispered.

"It was the only way to bring them all before Him. Deliver the oppressors to stand for judgment, and the innocent for mercy." Saying it out loud didn't make it sound any better after all this time, he knew that, but it was the only explanation he could give. "You have to understand that it made sense at the time, in some weird way. Even though we were going against Him, we did it for Him." Heaviness settled in his bones. "We killed them all in His name."

Coriander's voice was strained, breathy. "Was Lucifer really that convincing?"

Jude breathed out slowly. "Yeah. Yeah, he was. Once Lucius made the call, we descended. And we decimated them all." Regret was hollow in his throat as he continued, "There was so much blood, Cori. So much death. I hacked my way through those people. I was so angry. Angry at Him for leaving those people alone to suffer. Angry at the army that came for them. I was Vengeance. I was created for that purpose. And I unleashed devastation upon the city. I caused so much pain." Jude's voice broke on a cracked sob and Coriander snuggled closer, as if she could burrow underneath his skin. "I had eyes for nothing but rage and my own anger. I've never felt like that before."

Her lips were on his neck now, murmuring incoherent words on his skin, her hands moving over him in an attempt to soothe the fire burning within him.

"And when it was over, they were all dead. It was only us. Bloody and broken. And Lucifer was nowhere in sight, the sneaky bastard. Left us to fall all on our own."

"Is that why you can't touch people?" she asked quietly.

"Yeah." Jude gave a half-hearted laugh. "We each have our own cross to bear because of what happened. All the pain I caused those people, well, He made sure that I would never forget it. Every day, for the rest of my life, I have to live with the pain of their deaths." He snorted. "Probably a fitting punishment, but it sucks all the same."

Coriander skated her hand across his bare flesh and nipped underneath his jaw, the gesture beginning a slow burn in his blood. "So why doesn't it hurt when I touch you?"

He cradled her jaw in his hand and tipped her face up to his. "I don't know, Cori. I can't even question anymore."

"Faith?" She smiled. "Maybe?"

Jude shook his head. "No. I don't question, but that doesn't mean I have faith that there's anything good out there waiting for me. It hurts too much to hope at this point. So I don't. I can't believe in faith anymore."

"I believe in lots of things," Coriander said with a smile. "I don't think religion is as cut and dried as most people think. I think things like gods and angels exist in parameters that are predefined according to one purpose. His purpose. It doesn't make sense to me otherwise." She sniffed and leveled him with a penetrating stare. "I believe in a higher calling. I believe in power that I don't understand. I believe in you."

Jude's grin was playful. "Careful, Cori, you're skirting dangerous territory. Blasphemous, even."

"So says the man who uses the word 'fuck' like a comma," she smirked.

He sighed and pulled her closer, ignoring her huff of annoyance. "I remain true to myself, no matter what words I use."

"But you see my point. Sometimes you're not as angelic as you should be."

Jude's lips brushed hers with a feather-light kiss. "No. And I may not be a very good one, but I am an angel." A soft smile played at the edge of his mouth. "Which is more than I can say about you, princess."

For a second, an impish grin flashed across her face, allowing a glimpse of the carefree woman he loved to surface, despite her inner heartache. "Well," she drawled, "you may be right. But I do have my moments."

He bent to kiss her again. "Don't we all?"

Her fingers slid up his chest, pulling his shirt higher, and the blunt tips of her nails scraped over his nipple. Jude groaned as his eyes fluttered shut.

"But you don't have to wait anymore," she whispered. "For hope. Or faith. I'm right here. Believing in you."

He found it almost impossible to think of anything but kissing her when she looked at him that way, like the sun rose and set squarely on his shoulders. It was terrifying, being the focus of her earnest gaze, knowing her eyes were only for him. Terrifying, but exciting all the same.

The slow burn that pooled in his stomach whenever Coriander was around spread out across his limbs, and the only way he could think to get it to grow was to pull her closer and press his lips to hers. He wasn't disappointed.

She breathed a soft sigh into his mouth as she opened for him. Jude took the invitation and ran with it, groaning in pleasure as he tugged her across his body to lay her flat on the bed. The taste of her, like sunshine and sand, burst on his tongue, making him ache for more. He slanted his mouth to apply more heated pressure, urging her to open wider. He licked his way inside her mouth, searching out every corner, determined to map every inch of sweetness.

Coriander responded with enthusiasm, tugging up the hem of his shirt to slide her palms across his skin. He let go and shrugged off the fabric barrier, reaching for her shirt to return the favor. She unfastened the lacy scrap of her bra and tossed it to the floor, chuckling as she pulled him back down for a kiss. Her tongue trailed on the inside of his mouth as his hands shifted lower, making quick work of his jeans and boxers, and her cargo pants.

He wanted to go slow, to use his hands and mouth to tease and distract, to send her mind and her body into a state of pure pleasure. Jude knew Ashtiru's disappearance was the only thing at the forefront of her mind, but if he could give her something good, even for these few brief moments, all the heartache and uncertainty would be worth it. Yes, he was all for slow and sensual, gritting his teeth against the need to take her hard and fast and leave her breathless in his wake, but her tiny hands found his and guided them to her hips. She arched her body and tightened her fingers, urging him to grab hold of the edge of the matching lace panties.

"Off," she panted, her sweet breath spilling into his mouth.

With the one breathy word, his fingers dug into the lace, forcing them through the fabric. He yanked his hands apart, ripping them in two great tugs. Coriander cried out, high and sharp, and wound her arms around him as their lower halves finally met with nothing between them.

Soft and slow became a foreign concept, ludicrous even, under the circumstances. Her body writhed against his with purpose, the ripple of a woman trying to shake off her fear like a snake shedding a dead skin.

Jude's breath caught in his throat as she palmed his cock with quick strokes, the blunt edge of her nails slipping over the head. He groaned, capturing her mouth with a rough kiss. Coriander mouthed back with equal pressure, matching the bruising force with ardent pulls of her hand. Fire coiled at the base of his spine, tensing his muscles and breaking his concentration.

"Christ, Cori, keep that up and I won't last," he gasped.

Her throaty laugh rolled over him, dark and sweet with promise as she squeezed harder. "So get on with it."

He gave a rough snort to focus his efforts, and knocked her thighs open with his forearms, hooking her knees over his elbows. She stared up at him with eyes wide as moons, trust and faith reflected back at him with a force that threatened to shake him apart. Nothing registered but the feel of her skin on his and the tightness in his groin, leaving him rock hard and wanting. He nudged closer to her entrance, and threw his head back on a moan as he found her hot and wet and ready.

"Do it," she rasped. "Take me, Jude."

Her hands curled into his forearms, the short nails digging into his skin as he snapped his hips and entered her on a sharp thrust. She hissed, a low wail that turned into a heavy moan. The sound covered him in heat and need as he began to move. Jude's hands gripped her hips, anchoring her into the position, leaving her no room to do anything but hang on for the ride.

Coriander's body bucked, tight with tension, all fire and sizzle as he moved. The liquid heat of her body surrounded him, encasing him in warmth. Sweet sparks of electricity rippled through his muscles, running through his veins in a rush of desire. He thrust harder, each stroke a rapid-fire connection between their bodies, tying them together. Her head was thrown back, exposing the column of her neck as she uttered nonsensical groans and half-words out of a mouth slack with pleasure. The fullness of her kiss-swollen lips beckoned, and he leaned down, forcing more pressure upon her as he fastened his mouth to hers.

She was trapped tight beneath him, the shift of her body communicating a need for more. He eased back, snapping his hips in a punishing rhythm that sent shivers over his skin, making stars dance in front of his eyes. Coriander snorted, snuffling and gasping as she clawed at his arms. Her thighs quivered as her legs wrapped around him, drawing him deeper.

"Please," she whispered. "Please, Jude, please!"

He felt the tension in her body ratcheting higher, evident in the strain of her muscles as she shook around him. Jude's jaw clenched at the sensation, and he wanted nothing more in this moment than to take her over the edge with him. He barreled down on her, ignoring the blissful burning of the tattoo on his back. As much as he wanted to fly, he didn't want to do it without her. The pull of her body was strong, and he felt the electric coil of impending orgasm take hold.

Coriander vibrated beneath him, and he growled at the high-pitched mewling noises coming from her throat. She was close, and damned if he would lose it before he watched her come.

"Fuck, Cori. Come for me, baby." Jude ground his hips down, back and forth, slamming into her, ready to watch her go. Two more pounding strokes and she was gone, shouting his name like a benediction through her climax.

He rode her through the aftershocks, absorbing the tiny tremors that wracked her body. She was so beautiful, sweat-soaked and flushed, pleasure written across her every feature. Cat-green eyes fluttered open, fixing him with a sated gaze that snapped his last thread of control. Jude groaned out his release, rocking her body as he came, leaning into the clutch of her hands as she pulled him closer. The rush radiated from his core as he let it all go, feeling all of his emotions pour out through the aching pulse of his orgasm.

Jude's breath stuttered as he stilled, collapsing to the side of her. She didn't waste a second before snuggling into his chest, wrapping her arms around his waist. They lay there for several long moments, exchanging murmured endearments and lazy kisses as their breathing settled.

Her lips nuzzled into the crook of his neck. "What now?" she whispered.

Jude ran a smoothing hand over her hair and pressed a soft kiss to her head, keeping her tucked in the cocoon of his arms. "Sleep," he huffed. "Sleep now. Tomorrow we can make a plan."

"I can't do this without you."

His heart seized at her admission. He didn't want to think about what would happen if he failed her, and they were unable to bring Ash back home. It was a distinct possibility, but one that was best left unsaid. Instead he pulled her closer, throwing a leg over hers to anchor her to him. "I know, Cori. I know."

"Do you think he's making the right choice?" Elijah signed.

Mordecai shrugged. "Traipsing after her without the rest of us? No, I don't think so." He leaned back in the chair and closed his eyes. "We're a team, aren't we? We're supposed to do this together." The deaf angel blew out a low breath. "He'll fail. And then he'll die with her."

Elijah nudged him with a foot, making him reestablish eye contact. "What's wrong with that? Dying for the woman you love? It's a noble purpose."

He watched as Mordecai's eyes misted over with a haze of darkness. "It's a weakness. One that breaks the integrity of our strength as a group. We already have a purpose. It's not up to him to decide to change that," Mordecai said with quiet insistence. "There is nothing in this world that I could ever choose over you." Mordecai's gaze pinned him for a moment, then he got up and left the room.

Wide-eyed, Elijah stared at the empty space in the doorway, and wondered exactly which 'you' his brother meant.

CHAPTER NINE

Coriander stared at the phone in her hand, knowing she needed to push the button to initiate contact. So simple, yet she couldn't get her fingers to work. Avalon was the pinnacle of patience, almost as much as Persephone, but for some reason the thought of having to go over the enormity of the situation again stilled her fingers.

"You want me to call her?" Persephone's voice was soft and placating as she gingerly extracted the phone from Coriander's trembling hand.

Tears filled her eyes, the words stalling in her throat, and all she could do was nod as she relinquished her grip on the mobile device.

Persephone wrapped an arm around her and guided her to the sofa as she pushed a button, lifting the phone to her ear. "Hey, Lon, it's Seph. I'm here with Cori and Teir. We need you, hun."

Coriander let out a soft sob into Persephone's shoulder as they sat down.

"Yeah, it's urgent. Just get here and I'll explain everything." She paused, murmuring with a gentle nod. "As quick as you can. See you soon, love." Persephone hung up the phone and tossed it on the coffee table as she wrapped Coriander into her arms. "It's okay, Cori," she said softly. "Avalon's on her way."

"Is she?" Jude asked as he entered the living room.

"Should be tomorrow," Persephone said. "In the meantime," she looked at Coriander with fondness, "you should rest."

The redhead popped up from the sofa. "I can't. I need to get started." She held her hand out to her sister. "Teir's shit at research. You can help me until Avalon gets here. I've been thinking about the note, and I know he's referencing Meketaten and death, so the tomb makes sense. But it can't be that easy. I'm missing something."

Persephone clasped the offered hand and stood, nodding. "I don't know how much help I can be, but anything for Ash, you know that, Cori."

Coriander's face softened. "You just do what you always do, Sephie. Be here. Set things in motion. You're the best lucky charm there is. Good or bad."

"What do you want me to do?" Jude asked.

Her heart sank as she realized there wasn't anything the big angel could do. Not until she or Avalon figured out exactly where they needed to go. The earnest look in his eyes curled around her heart. He knew it, too. But he was still asking, still wanting to do anything. For her. For her child. Then it came to her.

"You know what you can do for me? For Ash?"

"Anything, Cori."

She pulled her bottom lip between her teeth, knowing she should hold her tongue and let it lie. But this was her baby out there, and she needed every scrap of hope and faith she could get her hands on. Asking him to do this was probably somewhere in the vicinity of asking him to forsake everything and fall all over again.

"Pray."

She saw the struggle in his face as he opened his mouth to speak. Finally, he managed, "I don't know if—I mean, it's—"

"She needs your prayers," Coriander said, cutting him off. "And I need my little girl. All you have to do is believe that. I'm not asking for anything else."

She tugged on Persephone's hand, not waiting for a response.

Avalon arrived on the red-eye, breezing into the house in the early dawn hours, sparing only a moment for a brief reunion with her sisters and an impromptu meet and greet with the angels, consisting mainly of attaching names to faces. Coriander's heart thumped in her chest as she watched her sister embrace Alex with a warm hug and gentle hand to his face. Avalon's honey-colored locks were pulled back into an efficient, yet messy bun, revealing an oval face with soothing brown eyes. She looked much the same as she always did; reserved, knowledgeable, and kind.

She spoke to Alex in a soft murmur before nodding at Coriander and disappearing into the library.

Two days later, she was still ensconced in heavy research, directing Coriander with firm and insistent instructions. One thing was for certain; Avalon knew her way around books.

Coriander pushed back the book in front of her with an indignant huff. "I don't think we're going to find anything. I can't waste anymore time," she said, shoving back from the table. "Jude and I will catch the next flight. We'll start at Luxor."

Avalon looked up from her notes with a glare. "You're rushing off, and you don't even know where, Cori. That won't do you any good if you have no idea where you should be looking." She walked over and pointed to a diagram in one of the open books. "Here. The tomb complex in Amarna. That's where Akhenaten was found. There are three side chambers, and it is speculated that Meketaten was buried in one of them. It's fact that remnants of her sarcophagus were found in the royal tomb."

Coriander sighed, leaning over the book. "I don't understand. It's recorded fact. Why would he take Ash here? Somewhere so easy to find? Somewhere already discovered?"

Avalon placed a hand over her arm. "I don't know. It is the most obvious. But what about the other side chambers? Is it possible that there's another that isn't recorded? We've been over all of this," she said, gesturing a hand to the pile of books, "and this has to be where he means." She shook her head. "The only possibility is another chamber. A secret chamber. That has to be it."

Coriander straightened. "It's about five hours to Amarna from Cairo. If we leave as soon as possible, that still gives us time. But what if we're wrong, and he's got her someplace else? What if he," her voice cracked, "kills her before I can get there? Before I can even try to exchange her for the amulet?"

Avalon's voice was gentle, but firm. "You don't have a choice."

"I'm scared, Lon. So fucking scared."

"Language," her sister huffed, sliding an arm around her. "We're all scared, sweetie. For you and for Ash. So go, but promise me you will stop and think before rushing off on a tangent." Avalon's arm tightened, pulling her closer. "You can do this. This is who you are. You find things. You'll find Ash. You'll bring her home."

Coriander wiped the tears that leaked from the corners of her eyes with the back of her hand. "Yeah," she sniffed. "We'll bring her home."

Coriander paused from her packing to look up and find Jude resting against the door frame, his arms crossed over his chest. "You packed?" she asked. "I'm just about ready to leave."

"Yeah, I'm good." He came inside and sat down at the foot of the bed, his expression quiet.

She kneeled down to reach underneath the bed, and pulled out a heavy lockbox, placing it next to her duffel. She fished the key out of the pocket of her cargo pants and unlocked the box, breathing out a heavy sigh as she picked up the amulet from its resting place.

"This is what he wants," she said softly, fastening the chain around her neck. "This is what he's willing to kill my baby for."

"Yes."

She sniffled, fighting back the tears that sprang to her eyes. "It's a demon, isn't it? This *man*, this thing—he's a demon, right?"

"Yes." Jude shifted back on the bed and crossed his ankles. "Not your garden variety, I'll give you that, but yes, probably a higher-ranking demon."

"Like the other one?" She couldn't bring herself to mention the whore's name. "The one who went after Seph?" Jude nodded. "Why?" she whispered. "Why is this happening?"

"I wish I knew," Jude said softly, reaching for her.

She allowed him to pull her close, winding her arms around his shoulders, letting her fingers dig into his skin as if she could draw his strength out through her fingertips. The contact was warm and comforting. He rested his head beneath her breasts, pressing his cheek to her abdomen.

"I'll give it up if I have to. If it means her life, I will."

Jude sighed against her and squeezed harder. "Do you know what it does? The amulet?"

"No." She pressed a kiss to the top of his head. "At this point, I don't even care. Nothing matters to me more than Ash."

He pulled back and stared up at her with a frown. "You can't give it up. We can't let them win. You said yourself you don't know what it does. All we know is that it's important to the Dark, important enough for them to use Ash as a bargaining chip. Have you given any thought as to why that is?

"I don't care. I just want her home."

His jaw tightened. "It must be powerful, " he said roughly. "Think, Cori. First, it's Persephone they want. Now, it's something connected with you—her sister. There's a bigger plan on the horizon and we have no idea what that is. We're behind the eight ball,and right now that thing around your neck is upping the stakes on a game we don't know the rules to."

She shook her head. "I told you I don't care about any of that."

His hands dug into her hips. "All I'm saying is that if push comes to shove and Ash is the difference between keeping that thing or letting them have it for Christ only knows what—" He broke off, closing his eyes for a moment. He breathed out slowly and looked back at her. "You just need to be prepared. In any eventuality."

Jude's words burned in her chest with an agonizing truth she couldn't bring herself to accept. Coriander let her hands fall from his neck and stepped back to glare at him. "He can't have Ash," she said through clenched teeth. "I don't care if I have to give up every relic I've ever found. I don't care if it wants to tear me limb from limb and roast me over open coals while jacking off over a Bible. I don't care if I have to sacrifice the lot of you at the feet of Satan himself." Her hands curled into fists. "My baby comes home."

He reached out and snagged her hand. "And I'm going to do my best to see that you both come home safe and sound. I just don't want you heading out into this without thinking about every possibility." Jude brought her hand to his cheek and leaned into her palm. "I've dealt with my fair share of the Brimstone Brigade and have seen firsthand how nasty it can get. I—"

"So have I."

His face twisted in confusion. "What?"

"Demons," she affirmed. "I've seen one before."

Jude pulled her down to sit beside him on the bed. "When?" he asked, taking her hands in his.

"A demon killed my parents."

The big angel's eyes went wide as his mouth fell open. "What?" he repeated. "Are—are you sure?"

"Sharp teeth, burning yellow eyes, out for blood? Ring a bell?" He nodded, dumbstruck. "I was little, three or four, out with my parents. It was dark and we were on our way home, just walking, when it came out of the shadows and tried to grab me." Coriander heard her voice go hollow as the memory returned. She swallowed. "It was awful. I remember screaming and my mother, my real mother, trying to push me behind her. It grabbed her and ripped her throat out. It all happened so fast—it was so loud, her screams, and my father yelling to draw its attention. It had giant claws and smelled like death." She paused and took a breath. "My father died screaming my name."

Jude's arm curled around her. "How did you survive?"

She lifted her face to crack a half-hearted smile. "Have you met Khemrhy?" Coriander's smile grew as she watched the recognition fall into place on his face. "She's one powerful lady."

"She saved you, then what? Took you home?"

Coriander nodded and sighed. "Yep. Like a stray cat. She saved us all, you know. Me, Persephone, Teraslynn, and Avalon. We're all orphans." She shrugged. "Well, were, at any rate. We're our own kind of family."

He chuckled. "I've noticed."

She stood up and zipped the duffel, shoving the lockbox back under the bed. "I can't promise anything," she said, looking him in the eye. "When it comes to Ashtiru, I'll do anything I have to in order to get her back."

Jude grabbed her face and pulled it down to his for a slow, tender kiss. When they broke apart, he rested his forehead on hers, breathing out softly over her parted lips. "I know. And I meant what I said. I'll do whatever it takes so that you don't have to." He kissed her again, a loud smack of lips on lips, and headed for the door. "I'll get my stuff. Meet you downstairs."

She watched him go and reached for the strap of the duffel bag, swinging it over her shoulder. He danced around it, but she knew what he was thinking. That if there was an exchange to be made, it wouldn't be a necklace for a live Ashtiru; it would be the other way around. Her hand curled over the amulet. If one hair was out of place on her little girl's head, then God help them all, because nothing would hold her back. Not demons. Not angels. Not the Almighty himself. Nothing.

Jude stepped off the landing into the living room to find all eyes staring at him. He squared his shoulders and gripped his bag tighter as he made his way to the front door. Winston stood by the door, crisp with propriety, but the older man's face was lined with sorrow.

"Your taxi is waiting, Master Jude."

He nodded as the three sisters rushed past him to attack Coriander as she descended the stairs. The women threw arms around one another in a barrage of hugs and kisses, the sounds of feminine voices echoing through the room. He turned back around to give them their moment when Lucius stepped in front of him, flanked by Mordecai and Elijah.

"Are you sure about this?" his leader asked. "If you want us to go with you, all you have to do is ask. We'll be there for you, you know that."

"Thanks, but I think you all know this ball game is mine to lose," Jude said. He cracked a wan smile. "And you know how I hate to lose."

Lucius nodded. "Just putting it out there."

"I know."

"I have—*We* have faith in you, brother," Lucius replied. "Just get back here in one piece, okay?"

"Yeah, about that. On the off chance I don't make it back...well, we had a good run, didn't we?"

"The best," Mordecai offered as Elijah shot him a thumbs up.

Jude grinned at them. "Boss," he said, turning to Lucius, "just so you know, if I had to do it all over again, I wouldn't change a thing. I'd follow you to the last, you know that, right?"

"Yeah," Lucius said. "Yeah, I know. Now get the hell out of here."

"Right," he said, moving to the door as Coriander came up behind him. Coriander had soft words and hugs for Lucius, Mordecai, and Elijah, before shuffling to enfold Winston in a giant embrace.

"Coriander." Alex's voice trembled as he stood up from the sofa. She turned, but did not go to him. "Bring her back." She gave him a stiff nod and went out through the open door.

Faint blue light pulsed over Alex's head, and Jude found his feet steering him in the direction of the Anubis. He came face to face with Alex, and for the first time, felt no animosity toward the tall, dark-haired man. Alex looked him over, assessing him before speaking.

"Promise me you'll bring them home," Alex said, his voice catching on the last word.

Jude grinned. "Only if you promise you'll never drop trou in front of me again." He let out a mock shudder. "Because no one should be subjected to that. Ever."

Alex chuckled as he offered his hand. "Deal."

Jude took it, gritting his teeth against the flash of pain that went up his forearm. He gave Alex a quick nod and followed Coriander outside. In a few hours, they would be on the ground in Egypt and the search would be on. He refused to look back at the house as they drove away, instead reaching out to clasp Coriander's hand. Jude brought it to his lips and kissed it, forcing the thought of everything but the feel of her skin out of his mind.

CHAPTER TEN

"This is not a hotel."

Jude stepped out of the cab and peered up at the giant edifice, the setting sun reflecting off the large beige stones.

"No, this is a market," Coriander answered, swinging her pack over her shoulder. "The Khan el-Khalili to be exact." She smiled at him, taking no note of the frown of displeasure on his face. "The largest in Cairo. I always find what I need here."

Jude adjusted the duffel in his grip and followed her as she walked inside. "I take it we need things?"

"We always need things, dear." He could hear the eye roll in her tone. She continued forward, the bright red of her ponytail swinging rhythmically from side to side as she walked.

He gritted his teeth against the sigh in her voice. "Look, if we're here so you can buy a toothbrush, I'm going to be very put out." She didn't answer. They passed stall after stall, each one overflowing with a myriad of merchandise from silk scarves to pottery to cell phones. She wove in and out of the crowd with purpose; she obviously knew her way around. Several of the stall owners paused in their sales pitches to flag her down, but she merely nodded and smiled, returning their beckoning hands with a wave of her own.

"I've got a toothbrush," she called back over her shoulder. "What I don't have is a gun. And neither do you. We're about to rectify that."

Jude grabbed her arm and pulled her back. "What?" He lowered his voice to hiss in her ear, "We're buying weapons?"

She blinked up at him. "Of course. There's no way either of us could have gotten them into the country. I told you I wasn't into smuggling." Coriander grasped his fingers and pried them loose from her arm. "Keep your panties on, sunshine. I've been doing business down here for years."

"Coriander," he warned. She waved him off.

"Don't 'Coriander' me," she shot back. "Or do you want to run off on this demon-killing spree with nothing but your bare hands?" Her eyes raked over him. "You can get away with the Bruty McBruteness act, but me, I need a piece. One that goes bang." He huffed and she continued, "I realize that you're used to staring them down with that scary expression of yours, but let's face it, I'm hardly intimidating. And nothing says 'Don't fuck with me' like a pair of hand cannons." She turned around and walked on, ducking into a side alley.

He followed her twists and turns past more stalls, and with each step he noticed the atmosphere changing. More people leaning out from doorways, casting furtive glances, speaking in hushed tones. They were veering off the beaten path. He made sure to keep his eyes on her at all times, just in case he needed to grab her and bust out with some of the McBruteness she accused him of a second ago.

Coriander slipped into another side street, and turned to knock with a light pattern of raps on a large wooden door. A square peephole covered with bars opened, and a man's voice murmured in Arabic. She spoke quickly, but with confidence, and in seconds he heard the sound of locks sliding back and the door opened. Coriander grabbed for his hand and pulled him inside.

A tall, thin Egyptian man dressed in jeans and a t-shirt shut the door behind him. He whirled on scuffed basketball shoes and gathered Coriander up in a gentle hug.

"Dr. Rhodes! A pleasure, a pleasure! What can Salih do for you this evening?" he asked in accented English.

She returned the hug and smiled. "Thank you, Salih. Do you have the usual?"

"Of course, of course. I keep an assortment on hand just for you. Only the finest for my Dr. Rhodes." He ushered them through a curtained archway. "Come through."

The room was small and sparse, with only two tables against the back wall. Woven carpets acted as tablecloths, and two boxes sat on the tabletop. Jude made out the barrels of several styles of guns sticking up.

"Please," Salih gestured to the boxes, "make your selections."

Jude's head reeled at the geniality of the tall man, offering Coriander her pick of firearms as if he were selling her something as mundane as a head wrap or home décor.

She wasted no time, diving right in to rifle through the goods with enthusiasm.

Jude's eyes narrowed as Coriander began to pile guns and knives on the second carpet-covered table, pausing every so often to lift a weapon into the air for inspection, as if she were checking fruit for blemishes. Salih nodded emphatically as she moved from item to item, no doubt calculating the final tally in his head with glee.

"Are you serious?" he hissed into her ear. "I mean, yes, *demons*, and all that, but don't you think this is a little much? Christ, I've been doing this for ages and have managed just fine with a pair of .45's."

She turned and flashed him a placating smile. "He has my baby," she countered, and he could see the anger and determination glittering in her eyes. "And when he sees you, there's no way he's going to pass up a shot at bagging himself a holy host." He pursed his lips in irritation as she continued, "So, there's you to consider as well. I have a dual need here to act upon this threat and protect that which I love." She patted him on the cheek as if he were Ashtiru. "And I do love you. I really do. It just so happens that demonstrating my love involves weapons. Lots of weapons."

Coriander turned back to the table and put her hands on her hips, surveying her choices. She shot Salih a bright smile. "We'll take these. Jude, pay the man."

Salih whipped out a beat-up calculator out of his back pocket and stabbed at the keys. It went on for what seemed like ages, and when Jude opened his mouth to protest, the Egyptian man shoved the calculator in his face.

"If it pleases you, Mr. Dr. Rhodes' friend."

Jude choked back a splutter at the figure on the screen, but at Coriander's harsh glare, dug out his wallet. "I assume you will accept American dollars?"

Salih nodded. "Of course."

He pulled out a wad of cash and pressed it into Salih's outstretched palm. "That should cover it."

Salih flipped through the bills and tucked them away before retrieving several boxes of ammunition and placing them on the table. He turned to Coriander. "With my compliments," he smiled. "Will there be anything else?"

"No, I think that should do it," Coriander replied, already packing away the purchases. "Thank you again, Salih. You're a lifesaver." She turned and presented Jude with two large, shiny guns. "45's, I believe you said."

He stayed quiet and sank to one knee, stowing the weapons in his bag. He zipped it up and rose to his feet, taking Coriander by the hand and leading her back out front. She said her goodbyes to Salih and once again they were back in the alley.

"Now what?" he asked her.

"Now we can go the hotel. If there's one thing I learned about Egypt, you never check in anywhere without protection."

"I hate Egypt."

Coriander raised a hand to her mouth in mock horror. "Take it back."

"No."

She snorted and poked him in the bicep. "And here I was thinking we could do a guided tour or something after we find Ash." She smiled at his frown. "Think about it, big guy. Endless dunes of sand, camel spit, not to mention the impromptu political coup. Fun and educational. What's not to love?"

He stared after her as she wound them back to the entrance and hailed a cab.

He shut the door of the room, dropping the bag off to the side, when he was suddenly face to face with a clinging Coriander. Her arms wrapped around his waist like bands of steel while she buried her face in the hollow of his throat, nipping and sucking with a frenzy. While her ministrations were causing interest in the lower half of his body, he grunted and managed to take hold of her upper arms and push her back.

"I know you want me," she rasped, eyes bright and glassy.

"Of course I do, but you need to sleep more than you need sex." It came out rougher than he'd intended, based on the way her spine snapped straight and her eyes darkened to points.

Coriander's face flushed deeper, the pink of arousal flooding to a raging shade of crimson. "Don't tell me what I need." She twitched in his grasp, and he wondered how long it would be before she tried to clock him one.

"Please," he said, switching tactics as he ushered her to the side of the bed. "Listen, for once. I know you're wound up and you want to get going, but there's nothing to be done about that tonight. It's blind frustration, Coriander, but you need rest to focus on tomorrow."

Her hands grabbed at him again. "What I need is for you to pound me into this mattress." She snaked her hands lower, fighting his fingers as she tried to get between his torso and the waistband of his jeans. "Come on, fuck me."

Jude stilled her hands and huffed out a breath of annoyance. "Not like this. Not now."

She snorted and launched herself at him again, latching onto his collarbone, biting down through the cotton of his t-shirt with purpose. "Why?" she whined.

The needy sound went straight to his groin, and he cursed under his breath at the traitorous jerk of his cock. Jude pulled her off and lowered his head to gaze directly into her eyes. "Because the next time I take you, it won't be because you're looking for a distraction. The next time I get you under me, I plan on making sure you know exactly why you're there." His hand brushed across the swell of her cheek, and her mouth parted as his fingers touched the corner of her mouth. "We're not going to fuck away your pain. I'm done with that." Her green eyes went wide and liquid with the admission. "I'm more interested in laying you down and giving you everything you've ever needed. And when I do, I promise I will do everything I can to please you. Not because you're trying to run away from something." His lips ghosted over hers with little more than a touch and a breath. "But because the chase is over."

A tiny gasp split her lips as she stepped back, her eyes misting over with a swirl of intensity. She rolled her bottom lip between her teeth and blinked long lashes at him, as if his words had finally registered.

"Say it."

With those two words, it was as if she'd ripped him open from stem to stern, leaving him to bleed out on the dingy carpet. His skin prickled with the sudden wash of exposure, running down his body like rivulets of sweat. There would be no greater moment, no better timing in all the universe, and he banished the thought that it was happening here at Christ only knew what time it was, in a seedy hotel room in the ass-back end of Egypt.

But it was perfect by all other estimations.

Jude stared into her face, drinking in the sight of her trembling lips and the delicate flutter of lashes as she tried to blink away the tears that formed in corner of her eyes. The realization that she was anything and everything to him, that she was tied into his soul in ways that could only be divine spread out over him like a shroud. He didn't know if it was faith or sheer, blind insanity, but whatever it was heated him from the inside out. It blossomed, coaxed into life as it crept through his blood to set down roots and grow.

"I love you."

Coriander launched herself into his arms again, pressing her lips to his in a forceful kiss that spoke of everything that had solidified between them. She buried her face in his neck and clung to him.

"Oh, God, I love you too," she whispered.

Jude set her back and smiled. "It was inevitable, wasn't it? I couldn't resist you if I tried."

She was beautiful as she smiled back. "But you tried very hard. It's commendable."

He rolled his eyes and pushed her toward the bed. "Change and get in there. I'm about to drop. We can discuss my valiant attempts at refusing your charms tomorrow, and you can mock me all you want."

"I would never do that." Coriander protested, and he glared at the innocent smirk plastered on her lips.

"Liar."

"On occasion."

He huffed at her light laugh, grateful to see the playful element to her personality returning bit by bit. She vacillated between highs and lows, her mercurial nature rising and falling like the tides. He meant it when he said he loved her, and somehow the rightness of expressing the sentiment settled into his heart with a swiftness that should have worried him. But watching her as she undressed and slipped under the covers, he realized there was really nothing to worry about on this particular front. All his worry and concern rested on the mission of bringing Ashtiru home and destroying the demon who would dare harm her.

Loving Coriander was the easy part. If only everything else was that simple. He could take it on faith that it would be, but it would take more than Coriander to make him believe it.

"I see you." The little girl's voice was hoarse in the darkness of the tent, sounding so much older than her precious few years. "I see him."

The Dealer snorted with derision. "Shut up."

She sniffled, the sound more in keeping with her youth, and he heard the scuffle of her feet as she tucked them beneath herself on the blanket. The shackles around her ankles clinked with the movement. Moonlight filtered in through the slit, illuminating the corner. Her eyes were cool and appraising, but she said no more. Curiosity got the better of him, and he asked, "Whom do you see, then?"

Ashtiru's eyes glittered and she smiled. "The lost one."

The Dealer turned away, unable to bear the frankness of her gaze. "We're all lost," he murmured to himself.

"You don't like him. No one does," she said with an air of finality. "But it doesn't matter."

"Really, my dear?" he asked on a sarcastic chuckle. "And why is that?"

Her bright laugh tinkled in the stillness, and he paled as the sound washed over him. A foul taste coated his tongue and he realized it was fear. He shook his head, unwilling to believe himself capable of the emotion when her next words hammered the point home.

"Because you won't ever see him again."

His hand rose up, and the little girl shrank back against her blankets, ducking her head. The flash of terror that crossed her eyes stayed his hand, and he lowered it slowly. He knelt down and leaned into her face, waiting for her to look at him. When her chin turned a fraction, he said, "Next time, I won't stop myself. Remember that."

Ashtiru sat up, and before he knew it, her tiny hands had latched onto his face, the green of her eyes receding to an inky blackness. He tried to jerk away, but she held him fast, forcing his gaze to hers. "I see all," she rasped, the age creeping back into her voice. "I see your death." The black of her pupils grew until all he could see was the swirling darkness, the whole of the universe roiling away within. Pinpricks of light, like the gathering of stars, winked back at him as a chill froze in his bones. Her fingers curled into little talons, and the ragged edges of her short nails bit into his skin. "You will fall," she whispered. "You will bleed on the golden edge of Vengeance, and your soul has been sold to bloody the hands of the beast."

The Dealer clamped down on her wrists, squeezing, sure her tiny bones would snap under the pressure. She held tight, her body giving no sign she registered his touch.

"Shut up!" he yelled, spittle flying out to hit her cheek.

Ashtiru continued, unfazed by his outburst, and her voice grew in cadence, rising in the air between them, "His mercy is eternal! His will is written across time! Vengeance is coming and he shall reap all the rewards of Heaven! You will fall!"

He wrenched her hands from his face and shoved her back. She scuttled backwards to the blankets and huddled underneath, the muffled sounds of crying filling the tent. He kept one eye on the huddled mass of little girl, and lowered the flame on the lantern, unwilling to banish the light entirely. He went back to his own pallet and pulled the cover aside. As he slipped under the blanket, a cold spike of fear traveled through his limbs, settling to fill his mouth with a metallic tang. He swiped a tongue over dry lips and realized he'd bitten it clean through.

It was several hours before he could tear his eyes away from her and fall into slumber.

CHAPTER ELEVEN

Elijah's jaw dropped. The tables once filled to almost toppling with leather-bound books were clear, their oiled wood shining in the wide open windows. He'd come looking for a reference inside a book on Egyptian hierarchy. It was not on the table where he'd left it. Elijah noted all books were neatly on the hardwood shelves. As he quietly walked over to a shelf and looked at it, mouthing the titles, he began pulling books for his own reading pleasure.

"You! What are you doing?" came a sweetly feminine voice from behind him, "Put those back!" Elijah turned and his jaw dropped open to gape. She was beautiful, standing in the glittering sun. Her sleek brown hair was piled up in a messy ponytail, a lock fallen over her glasses. He fought the urge to reach out and brush it behind her pert little ear. She slapped a dusty hand on her jean-clad thigh, making a puff of dirt rise up. She sneezed hard as Elijah's fingers fumbled, trying to find the words to tell her why he was there. She stared at him hard, her brown eyes unyielding.

Elijah signed, "I'm here for a book."

"Oh, you're deaf. Do you read lips?" she said as she cocked her head. Elijah shook his head and arched and eyebrow as he raised his hand to his throat and held it out to her.

She leaned in and said loudly, "I'm Avalon. Av-A-Lon. What are you looking for?"

Elijah felt dumbstruck at that moment. He leaned his head forward, almost close enough to kiss her. She leaned back and frowned, "Oh, bother. I'll get some paper and a pen. Just a second." Avalon turned, and with a swish of her hips, she was gone amidst the shelves.

Elijah took that moment to sign, "I'm sorry if I messed up your books. I can't talk to you." He stared at his hands and sighed. "Useless," he mouthed. His eyes shot open wide as he looked around for a witness. Avalon came back, her hair arranged a little less messy, a pad of paper and a pen in her hand.

He took the pad and pen and scrawled out a quick, "Not deaf, mute. I hear you fine. Can't speak."

She blushed as she peeked over his hands at the pad, pink creeping into the golden tinge of her skin. "Ah, I see. Sorry."

He waved a dismissive hand and smiled back at her before scribbling again. "It's okay. Do you sign?"

"Not well." She shrugged her shoulders.

He felt like an idiot, standing there, grinning at her. *Wonderful.*

Alex awoke to the brightness of sunlight, tangled in sheets and sweat. The scent of sand and spice filled his nostrils as he sat upright and raked a hand through his dampened curls. It was no use fighting any longe. The pull was insistent now, unwilling to be ignored. He dressed in silence and packed his bag. He was only a day behind Coriander and the big angel. It wouldn't be too hard to track them down.

He pulled out his mobile and dialed. "Nico, it's Alex. I need you to get me on the next flight to Cairo." He paused, flinching at the litany of rapid-fire Greek on the other end of the line. "Look," he interjected, "just do it, okay? I'm headed out to the airport now." He nodded.

"Thanks. I owe you one." He ended the call and pocketed the phone before picking up his bag, heading downstairs.

The rest of the house was quiet, the lingering traces of sorrow clinging to every surface like a film. The house, full of people, was still and empty without Ashtiru's presence. The weight of duty was heavy as he descended the staircase. He knew what he was leaving behind as surely as he knew what waited for him in the distance. A half-hearted smile graced Alex's lips. Maybe one day Coriander would understand. He certainly wasn't going to get the chance to explain it to her.

"You're leaving."

Alex lifted his hand from the doorknob and whipped his head around to stare at Lucius. "Yeah."

"Change your mind, then?"

"Something like that."

"I trust him, you know. Jude," Lucius clarified.

He sighed, taking the bag in both hands. "So do I."

"But not enough to think he can do it on his own." Lucius' lips flattened to a tight line.

"That isn't the case," Alex said softly. "This is my child we're talking about. I meant it when I said I couldn't go, but..." His voice trailed off as Lucius nodded.

"You're her father." The angel's eyes were sober with compassion.

"Yes. Some priorities take precedence."

"Some things are greater than death."

The statement hung in the air, latching onto his skin. Alex swallowed and nodded. "Then you know."

"I suspected as much. I'm actually much smarter than they give me credit for." Lucius smiled with warmth. "The technicalities involved in the lives of deities are complex, but in the end, it all comes back to death. It's pretty morbid, really."

Alex chuckled. "I've been running a long time. Afraid of what would come." Blue light misted over him and he pointed to the faint sparkle. "I can't run anymore."

"A brave sentiment."

"A guilty conscience."

"He will bring them home."

"We're not talking about the same 'he', are we?"

Lucius took in a deep breath and let it out with purpose, fixing him with his gaze. "Our will is His will. And it has already been written. All that's left is to carry it out. That's what we do. You, me. All of us."

"Are you saying that what I do doesn't matter, because it's already been predestined?" He couldn't help the twinge of annoyance that colored his words. "I could choose not to go. Choose of my own free will. Are you saying that has no effect on the outcome?"

"No," Lucius offered, "I'm saying that even if you choose not to go, the end result will be to His design. Do you trust Him?"

Warmth spread through Alex, and this time he knew who Lucius meant. "With my life. It's all I have."

Lucius nodded. "It's all any of us have. And your life is in His hands. Mine too. That comforts me. I hope it comforts you."

"I'm scared shitless."

"Then you know you're on the right track." Lucius pushed off from the arm of the sofa and walked over to extend his hand. "Godspeed."

Alex clasped the angel's large hand and shook it. "Thank you."

He was halfway out the door when he turned back to Lucius.

"Can you do something for me, Lucius?"

"Anything I can."

"Pray for me."

A warm smile split the angel's features. "You know I will."

Sanjeev said nothing as she pulled the door open to allow Alex entry. "The mistress is upstairs." She shut the door behind him and moved to guide him to the stairs.

"I remember the way."

Her lips tightened, and she looked him over with a thorough rake of knowing eyes. Sanjeev breathed out in a small huff before nodding. Her slippers whispered softly on the tile as she left him alone.

Alex ascended the stairs and found himself in front of Khemrhy's door. He knocked twice and waited for a reply.

"Come."

She sat in a high-backed chair at the far end of the bedroom. Khemrhy placed the book she was reading on the little table next to her, and untucked her feet, letting them rest gently on the carpet.

"I wondered how long it would take for you to come to me." He didn't like the assumption in her words, even if there was no malice behind them.

"What made you so sure I would come?" he asked.

"Because I know you. I know what you are."

He snorted on a laugh. "Pull the other one, it's got bells." Khemrhy rolled her eyes and gave a dismissive shake of her head. He paused, waiting for her to say something. When it was obvious she planned to remain silent, he said, "I guess I'm supposed to ask. What am I, then?"

Her hands folded in her lap, the delicate fingers lacing together as she smiled. "A father."

"Then you know why I'm here."

"Of course I do. I know many things." She gestured to the chair on the opposite side of the table. "Sit. We shall talk."

He shook his head. He'd already wasted enough time, and talking through his issues at the moment turned his stomach. "No. I don't want to talk."

"Not even a little?" Her face was gentle and soft, in that innate way of mothers.

"I have to go. I can't fight it." The words felt hollow on his tongue. "I told myself I couldn't go at first, and that felt right, but now —"

"But now you have to go," she finished. "And you know what going back means."

He shifted on his feet, feeling restless in his own skin. Khemhry had a way of doing that to people. Whenever he was in her presence, he found it irritating, like there wasn't anything he could hide from her. She had a way of drawing out the things he pushed to the back of his mind, things he didn't want anyone else to know. Not even Coriander. It had to be some sort of divine by-product. But Khemrhy hadn't been truly divine in a long time.

"I'm going to die."

"Everyone does."

"Don't," he snarled, raking a frustrated hand through his hair. "Don't give me platitudes. You know what I'm facing."

Her eyes flashed and she unfolded her hands to rest them on the arms of the chair. "Watch your tongue."

"Then don't talk down to me. If nothing else, I deserve a little of your respect for what I'm about to do." The knot in his gut twisted, and he wanted to close his eyes against the sensation. Too many emotions were coming at him at once, assailing him from all sides, making it harder and harder to stand upright.

Khemrhy stood up, her tiny hands clenched into fists. "If you think I'm going to stop you, you're mistaken. You forget this is a path of which I am not afraid. Death does not frighten me."

"Well, it scares the hell out of me."

She laughed, and the tension eased out of her body. "Oh, Alex," she said softly. "You've faced far worse than death in your life. How you've managed to stay alive this long is a mystery even to me."

"Danger, yes. I can live with danger. A narrow miss near the Strait of Gibraltar, a pair of two-faced dealers in Lisbon, and getting unwittingly involved in a turf war in Morocco. That I can handle. This—" He let out a low breath. "I know I'm not coming back. What if—"

"No 'what ifs'. There is only 'what will be'." She came forward and took his hand, squeezing with gentle pressure. "There is this life. And the next. How or when we get there is not for us to decide."

He felt himself trembling, and was surprised to feel the smaller woman curl her arms around his waist. She was warm and soft and comforting. "Will they be alright?" It came out less manly than he intended, more broken and scared. Khemrhy squeezed tighter in reassurance.

"Ashtiru will be fine. She is young and is far more resilient."

"And Cori?"

Khemhry stepped back and placed a hand on his chest. "Coriander will do as she has always done."

"That's what I'm afraid of."

"No, it isn't. You want to know if she's going to miss you. If she's going to regret not loving you the way you love her." Her eyes were sad and understanding. "And the answer is yes, she will miss you. No, she will regret nothing."

Alex nodded, the truth stinging even though he already knew the answer. "Will he make her happy?" he asked, knowing full well the goddess knew exactly who he meant.

Khemrhy's smile was sly and full of motherly love. "If he doesn't, he will answer to me. But it seems as though you've already given him your blessing."

"I have."

Her eyebrow arched and she tilted head her to the side. "Then what are you waiting for?"

The words resonated in his chest as he spoke. "You are Death. I'm waiting for yours."

Khemrhy sighed, running a hand through her hair as she turned from Alex and went to the door. Her shoulders felt heavy as she reached for the doorknob, a mild flutter of panic racing through to her heart. She shoved the feeling to the back of her mind and entered.

The room was truly endless, and black as pitch. Sand whispered beneath her feet as she walked to a wall and pulled a cloak, dark as a starless night, from a peg. Everything died, she reminded herself as she pinned the cloak at her throat. Alex was strong. The truth in his heart had been weighed ages ago, and if he was feeling the calling now, then it meant he was ready. Whether or not he wanted to accept it. It was not her place to judge. It was her place to guide. The blessing was all she had to give. And she would give it freely and without prejudice. As always, death remained the ultimate equalizer. It cared not for rich or poor, weak or powerful. She was faithful. She would do her duty. It was up to Alex to accomplish the rest. Power flared to life as she raised the hood over her head, and turned and left the room.

Alex watched with teary eyes, feeling the blue nimbus of light pulse in recognition as the goddess Khemrhryia stepped out of the room. She was tiny, so easily unnoticed as she drifted to him. Her hand was cool where it cupped his cheek, her thumb soft as it brushed a stray tear.

The goddess's voice was a whisper when she spoke. "We all hear the Creator at two times. When we are born, he welcomes us into the world and out of the chaos, and when we are to die." A faint buzzing sounded in his ears, and he felt his body shudder under an unknown weight. Her hand lowered and heaviness crept into her tone. "I shall miss you, my friend."

CHAPTER TWELVE

Jude blinked into the sunlight, raising a hand to shield his eyes from the glare. A rough poke to his back got his attention.

"Here," Coriander said, thrusting a pair of sunglasses into his hands. "I realize they're not nearly as imposing as those damn Gargoyles that Dom wears, but they're functional at least. The sand can be blinding even when the sun's not overhead."

"I'm no stranger to sand, love," he said, putting the glasses on. "I've been around long enough to see cities sprout up from the desert itself." Jude snorted. "Not nearly as colorful as it used to be." He raised his chin and looked out over the sprawling dunes. "I seem to remember a lot more blue. And aurochs." He smiled and tilted his head. "Seen any aurochs in your adventures?"

Coriander's lips pursed in a glaring pout. "Really? You want to date yourself with an extinct species of cattle and a demoted Wonder of the World? You know how I feel about these things. It would hurt less if you stabbed me or something."

"I don't see why me taking a couple of pot-shots at the Ishtar Gate has you in such an uproar. It's not like I wasn't there when it went up or anything," Jude protested. "I distinctly remember disliking Assyria for some reason."

Coriander frowned, and damned if the little furrows in her brow didn't go straight to his gut and start burning.

"Babylon," she bit out through clenched teeth.

Jude smiled, enjoying the pleasant sensation of basking in her irritation. He waved a dismissive hand in the air. "Whatever. Assyria, Babylon, Sumer. It's all the same. Oppressively hot with a side of sand and unrest."

She hefted her pack higher on her shoulder and walked on, blatantly ignoring him. He followed her to the edge of the square as it fanned out into more dunes and asphalt-covered byways. He watched as her arm sailed in the air to flag down a passing truck. It slowed to a halt, and she jogged over to lean in the passenger window, speaking rapidly to the driver. Coriander turned back and waved him over, flashing a bright smile.

"We're in luck. They're headed to Luxor and will be happy to drop us in Amarna." She reached into the pocket of her cargo pants and pulled out a wad of cash, slipping it to the man in the passenger seat. He counted it briefly and motioned for her to get in. "Come on," Coriander called. "Hop in."

Jude climbed in behind her and settled down. She popped a tiny arm over the side and rapped twice on the side of the truck. The ancient vehicle groaned as the driver put it in gear and they sped off, Coriander's laughter ringing in his ears.

The bustle of Cairo melted away under a shimmer of heat in the distance, giving way to the stark desolation of high, empty dunes. Memories poured back into his brain, desperate and hateful, and Jude had to close his eyes behind the shades to get his world to stop spinning.

"You need this," Coriander called out over the wind, slapping a tube in his hand. "I realize that while you're all golden and gorgeous, without sunscreen, even you will burn, pretty boy."

She had a pool of white goo in her other hand and was rubbing it vigorously on the pale expanses of her exposed skin. Rather than argue with her, he flipped the cap open and squirted a palmful in his hand. As he finished applying the cream, he rubbed the excess off on his pants, only to find her beaming back at him with something else in her hands. She leaned up and jerked the baseball cap onto his head. He pulled the sunglasses down and glared at her.

She shrugged, smirking. "Scalp burn is a bitch," she said with cheer as she pulled another one from the pack and put it on, pulling her ponytail through the back.

Even with the heat, the wind was sharp and biting, and she snuggled closer into the crook of his arm. "Relax," she said. "We'll be there in a few hours. In the meantime, enjoy the scenery."

Jude rolled his eyes and pressed a kiss to her hat-covered head. She hooked an arm through his, and he settled back with a sigh. Soaking up these next few hours on the open road would probably be as close to intimate as they would get for the foreseeable future. He cleared his head and allowed himself to be lost in the desert.

His eyelids fluttered open as the truck shuddered to a stop. Coriander stirred next to him, reaching up to place a soft kiss on his cheek.

"We're here, sleepyhead. Did I lose you to the desert already?"

Jude grunted as he grabbed their bags and climbed out of the bed of the truck. She hopped down after him and headed around to the driver's side door, offering him her thanks and a hearty handshake. Jude held up a hand to shield his nose from the kick-up of sand as the truck rolled off down the road. As the dust settled, he could see the outskirts of the city ahead, flanked in the distance by the outcropping of ruins and tumbling monoliths.

He lowered his arm, and Coriander slipped her hand into his, squeezing softly. "Isn't it beautiful?" Her voice held a touch of wistful nostalgia. He looked down at her and squeezed back.

"Yeah," he managed, not looking at the scenery. "Beautiful."

Her resultant blush pinked her cheeks through the slight windburn. "Stop it," she chided. "Let's go." She took off, dragging him along toward the slivers of civilization.

The horizon was dappled in shades of orange and gray as the sun dipped lower. Night was coming. And where night came, demons followed. Jude stiffened.

"Sun's going down. It will be dark soon," she said. "That will be our best chance to slip in." She pointed in the distance. "The tomb complex is this way. It should be full dark by the time we get there."

"You know what that means, don't you?" he asked.

Coriander nodded. "I do. But I'm ready. And I'm here. I refuse to wait any longer. Every moment we wait, Ash could still be in danger. I'll be in that tomb before he can lay a finger on her." She dropped his hand and headed off.

"Wait!" he called after her. "You can't just go charging into pyramids, Coriander. We need a plan. I know it's hard, but try to look at this rationally-"

His words cut off as she shoved him roughly and he tumbled backwards to land on his ass in the sand. Fire blazed in her eyes as she scooped up a handful of sand and threw it at his head. He spluttered, shaking the grit out of his hair, and swore loudly.

"Just what do you think you're doing?" Jude growled.

Her impertinence was back in spades as she shifted the pack onto her shoulder and planted her hands on her hips. "I've just moved heaven and earth, you giant ass. Now, let's go find my baby."

He got to his feet and grabbed his bag to trail after her. As Amarna loomed in the distance, the chasm in his gut grew wider. The sun continued to set, turning the sky in swirls of orange and purple. As they came closer, they bypassed the city streets, winding their way through side paths and covered walkways, until at last, the tomb complex came into full view. Here, the desert sprawled, wide and open, behind the tiny constructs of somewhat-modern civilization, and the ancient pull of dunes and gods beckoned underneath the darkened sky. They trudged along in silence, and as the last rays of sunlight dipped on the horizon, Jude's fingers reached out for her. Coriander's hand slipped into his with a light squeeze. He smiled at the flutter in his chest and walked on.

The warm wind that had been circulating had grown cooler with the onset of night, as stars peeked out and twinkled against the inky backdrop of the heavens.

Jude raised his head to peer up at the crumbling stones. "Are we going to just walk right in?"

Coriander stopped, adjusting the backpack, before turning her head to survey the area. She frowned. "I don't understand. We shouldn't have been able to get this close without spotting a guard or two. I mean, it's not Fort Knox, but they're pretty vigilant about keeping people out after dark."

The wind stilled and the tiny hairs on the back of Jude's neck prickled to attention. This was wrong. There was something off. He instinctively reached for Coriander to draw her back, but she slipped free of him and trotted forward instead.

"Cori, wait! Let me at least take a look around-"

Jude's words cut off as the scent of sulfur washed over him. *Brimstone. Demons.* And they were out in the open.

He dropped to one knee and scrambled to dig out one of the .45s. Gun in hand, Jude was back on his feet just in time to hear Coriander scream into the darkness.

"Cori!" he yelled, taking off to the sound of her voice. His steps brought him close to the tomb complex. He felt the edges of the edifice looming in the distance even if he couldn't see it yet. But no Coriander. "Cori!" he called again, louder this time, and the only rejoinder was the sound of evil hissing.

Yellow points of light peeked out the darkness, and the brief glimpse was enough to put him headed in the right direction. He shot forward when they disappeared. Jude stumbled ahead, throwing the pack over his shoulder and steadying the .45 with both hands. As he got closer, his night vision improved somewhat, allowing him to see the outlines of stone in the dark. Coriander's name was on the tip of his tongue and he wanted to yell for her again, but he kept quiet, lest he give away his position.

He faltered as he hit steps, ascending slowly, the gun trained downward. If he popped one off accidentally, he ran the risk of hitting Coriander. He knew from experience that demons had no qualms about using humans as shields, and blowing a hole in Coriander would definitely put a damper on his endgame of getting them all back alive. They were alone here, and without Elijah to heal, injuries needed to be kept to a minimum.

Jude breached a doorway, slipping further into the blackness. It was cooler inside, and the scent of sulfur was now tinged with the smell of old sand and the heavy cling of ancient musk. A scraping noise ahead brought his head up at an angle as his ears craned to pinpoint the sound. He heard muffled words and the shuffle of bodies, and his eyes narrowed as he realized what was happening. He was being lured. It was using Coriander, stifling her cries just enough to keep him moving. There was no doubt it was a trap, and he was following along as planned. The scant hint of a smile curled the corner of his lips. This was a game he knew well.

Jude wondered how the demon would react when it realized the hunted was hunting the hunter.

He needed light. With light came shadows, and with shadows, he had the opportunity to conceal himself and better his advantage. There was no telling how much farther ahead they were, but since it was drawing him in, it wouldn't be by much. If it were him, he'd want enough distance to see an attack coming, but not enough to lose sight of his prey completely. Demons were often slow on the uptake, but they were killing machines and not to be underestimated.

Jude blinked twice into the darkness, focusing his eyes on the rough outline of the walls. His nostrils twitched as something new filtered in over the sulfur and sand.

Kerosene. Bingo.

Carefully, he shifted his weight back, making sure his feet didn't scrape on the floor. He moved until his back rested against the wall. He eased down to a crouch, setting down the pack. His fingers maneuvered the zipper and reached inside, finally digging around to curl around his cell phone.

He pulled it out and tapped the power button, coaxing the screen to life. His hand swept out, the dim light arcing around the room long enough for him to find the source of the fuel smell. A forgotten kerosene lantern sat in the corner across the room on its side, the flammable liquid seeping out onto the floor. Jude shut the phone off and jammed it in his pocket, reaching back in the bag. He set the gun down and pulled out the box of matches from the bottom of the bag.

Jude took a deep breath, centered himself, and lit a match, tossing it across the way and retrieving the .45 in one go. Flames erupted from the corner of the room, bathing the chamber in flickering light. He whirled around the doorway, back out into the opening, and peeked his head around. The demon came into view, and the minute Coriander laid eyes on him she began to struggle.

It growled, pressing its hand across her mouth, but the firelight gave him the opening he needed.

"Down, Cori!" he yelled, and she thrust her elbow back sharply, making the demon falter and lose its hold. She dropped to the ground and Jude raised the .45, squeezing off one shot. The demon's head exploded in a shower of gore, and crumpled to the ground.

Coriander cried out as bits of the demon made contact with her skin. He knew how it burned, and lurched forward to grab at her and pull her away from the corpse.

"Christ, that hurts!" she howled.

Jude pulled out the bottle of water, muttered a few words and unscrewed the cap, and poured it over her. She sighed with evident relief.

Coriander raked her hands down her arms, ridding herself of the excess water. "What is that? Just water?"

"Sort of. It's holy water."

She stared at him. "When in the hell did you get holy water?"

"Just now," he said with a smile. "I may have blessed it before I drenched you."

"Well, isn't that handy?" she huffed.

Jude shrugged. "It's been useful on occasion."

Coriander wiped her hands over her face and squeezed out her ponytail. "Come on, then. Let's go further." She glanced at the muck on the ground. "I think we're on the right track."

He grabbed the pack and eased her away from the dying flames. Coriander grabbed for his hand and led the way, slinking around corners with a sure-footedness that made him wonder if she didn't have the layout etched in her brain. Scattered along the walls, small torches were lit, reaffirming the notion that someone or something was definitely expecting them.

Alex stepped off the plane onto the jet-way, ignoring the itching at the base of his skull. He tightened his grip on his bag and walked into the terminal, passing easily through the thinning crowd. When he made his way out of the airport to the rental car stand, the itching subsided, replaced by a dull ache in the center of his chest once his feet hit the concrete outside. *Damn.* It was beginning.

He swallowed, pushing aside the fear and apprehension, and forced himself to focus on an image of little Ashtiru's face. Each step weighed heavier and heavier, and by the time he unlocked the car, his heart felt like a rock lodged in his sternum. Somewhere within, the jackal growled in response. Alex raked a hand through his hair as he slid into the sedan, taking a deep breath as he curled his fingers around the steering wheel.

Images assaulted him and he closed his eyes, unable and unwilling to sort through them for clarity. Lives passed him by in flashes. Birth and death, love and war, rage and anger, all wrapped in burning sands and the convictions of faith that didn't belong to him. Before he could take another moment to process it all, he turned the key and threw the car into gear, pealing out in a squeal of tires. He didn't dare try to figure it out now. It was far too late for that. The only thing he could do now was follow his instincts, and hope like hell it was going to be enough to save his child.

The jackal growled again, and Alex turned the car south for Amarna.

Jude followed behind Coriander, the glow of her flashlight adding more light to their path as it mixed with the interspersed torches on the walls. She ducked into a side alcove and pulled him inside, her breath catching as the beam of the flashlight hit the edge of a large object in the center of the room.

"Is that what I think it is?" he asked.

"Don't tell me this creeps you out?" she snorted as her eyes scanned the hieroglyphics on the walls. "But yes, this is a tomb."

"Wonderful. Anybody I know?" he quipped.

"I don't think so," Coriander snapped. "Unless you're long lost pen pals with Setepenre."

"Who?"

He heard the eye roll in her huff of escaped breath as she examined the wall further. "Setepenre. One of Akhenaten's daughters, sister to Meketaten." Coriander turned to face him. "She died before her sister, so most likely we need to go further in."

Jude glanced at the object. "And is that, you know, *her*?" He gestured at the sarcophagus.

"Doubtful," she replied. "The body is probably long gone, but yeah," she squinted at the rectangular stone tomb, "that looks like it could be hers."

"Think there's anything useful inside?" Jude curled his hands on the edge of the sarcophagus, ready to push it open.

"Don't!" Coriander cried. "Don't open it! You'll-"

"What?" he shot back, crossing his arms over his chest. "Please don't tell me you were going to use the word 'desecrate' in reference to me." The big angel smirked. "Please."

Her face scrunched up, disgruntled. "Fine. But can't you bless it first or something?"

"I'm not the Pope, Coriander. Water is the extent of my purview." Jude glanced down at the hieroglyphics carved into the lid. "And I don't think this chick is Catholic." Ignoring the squeak of protest from Coriander, Jude pushed against the lid, and it groaned with the friction of stone on stone as it moved.

"Jude," she warned. "This is not a good idea."

He grunted and put his back into it, shoving harder. "What do you mean? I thought this would be right up your alley." Sweat beaded on his forehead and he grinned at her. "Isn't this what you do?"

Her hands planted on her hips and she frowned. "No!" she shouted. "I mean, yes, but not like this! You don't know what could happen when you touch-"

A louder creak of moving stone made her head snap up and her face go white. Jude paid no attention to the fluttering of her hands as she tried to stop him, and pushed the lid off the top by a few inches, enough for a smattering of dust to waft up from the interior.

"Jude," she said again, her voice more insistent.

"Hang on, I've almost got it off."

"*Jude.*"

"What?" he snapped, straightening.

"Oh, you idiot!" she cried, grabbing at him and running for the opening, which was swiftly closing behind the appearance of a hidden door.

Coriander pulled her fingers back just in time before it shut with a loud thud, trapping them inside. She whirled around on him with a murderous glare. "You feather-brained moron! Look what you've done!"

He swallowed sheepishly. "Sorry."

She closed her eyes for a second and drew in a calming breath.

"I really am sorry."

"I know. It's fine," she said, tapping her finger on her cheek. "Give me a second. I need to think."

The horror of the situation finally dawned on him, and a tiny flutter of panic settled in his throat. Coriander, on the other hand, had relaxed, all traces of her earlier ire gone, her features set in concentration.

"Oh, God," he groaned as his eyes darted around the room. "Oh, shit. Shit, shit, shit."

"Unclench, sunshine."

"We're trapped in a tomb, Coriander! How can you be this calm?" Jude bellowed.

She gave him a bright smile and knelt down, digging though her bag. "Happens to me all the time. No big deal, we'll just...work around it. I'm sure you've been in worse scrapes before." She waved her hand, blowing him off. "Fiery demons and the whole twelve circles of hell are a lot more complicated than the tomb of a lesser known Egyptian princess, I'm sure."

"Nine," he frowned. "It's nine, and I would rather be taking tea in any of them than sitting here on my ass while you try to MacGyver us out of this with a roll of duct tape and some incense!" Jude rubbed a defeated hand over his face and rolled his eyes skyward. "Why do you do this to me?"

Coriander's bright smile widened. "Because, big guy, some days you're the pigeon, and some days you're the statue. And with a butt like that," she said, smirking at his rear, "expect some shit. Besides, I told you not to touch it."

Hours passed as Jude watched Coriander trace the perimeter of the chamber over and over again, scrutinizing the carvings on the walls. She murmured under her breath every so often, stopping to check and recheck panels of stone he knew she probably had memorized by now. He checked his watch again for the fourth time in the last ten minutes, his patience having ramped from manageable to hell and gone in the space of the last hour. His irritation finally got the better of him, and he stood up and brushed himself off.

"There's got to be a way out."

"There isn't."

"There has to be," he scoffed. "I mean, when they were building this thing, if you got trapped inside-"

"Then it's 'Welcome to the Rest of Your Afterlife'. It's a tomb, Jude, not a Motel 6. You check in. You don't check out."

Jude leaned against the rough stone wall and crossed his arms, scrutinizing the other side of the tomb as she returned her attention to the duffel. "So, if there's no way out, how do you propose we get out of here, Indiana?

You got a spare skeleton key in your purse? Or were you just planning on me pulling a Superman and busting through that wall over there?"

The stiffening of Coriander's spine caught his eye as she paused from rifling through her bag. She stood up with a slow ease and turned to face him, the glow of the lantern light casting shadows across her lovely face. Her lovely, pissed-off face.

She came to stand in front of him and held up a hand in his face, all five fingers splayed wide for him to see.

"One," she said, folding her thumb into her palm, "We've had the discussion regarding you comparing me to fictional archaeologists and glorified treasure hunters, so cut it out. Two," she folded down her index finger, "It's not a purse, it's a satchel. It carries more important things than tampons and lip gloss. Things that will most likely end up saving your feathery ass. Three," the middle finger came down, "If you want to play Superman, be my guest, but these walls are over thirty feet thick in places, and while I do not doubt your ability to smash through them like a horny musk ox on a rampage, they will hit back. And you, big guy, are without a healer." The ring finger came down and she fixed him with a penetrating stare. "Four. If you can remember how it feels to have faith, have a little in me now. I got this. It's what I do."

"And five?"

She folded her pinky down, making the tight fist. The quick jab to the midsection was only hard enough to make him smile.

"That was five, jackass," she smirked, "Now quit second-guessing me and stay out of my way. I'm about to amaze you."

He just shook his head. *Been there, done that, bought the fucking T-shirt.* "Why do I feel like every day with you is a Spielberg film?"

"I don't know," she answered, pulling a small brush from her satchel and taking the flashlight to the wall. She brushed dust and dirt away from the carvings, and her lips moved as she read. Shadows crossed her line of sight and she huffed, "Can you please move your heft? Your abs of steel are blocking my light. Yes," she hissed as he moved and the darkness receded. She peered closer at the wall. "This is it. The answer is here." She tucked the brush away and started to feel the hieroglyphics gingerly with her fingers. "And quit with the drama queen theatrics, you big baby. I mean, no sharks, no Nazis, no pirate ships, no aliens, no...no, no *sharks*."

"Let me put this in terms you can understand, Coriander."

She turned around, and the annoyed glare in her eyes made him smile.

"What?"

His grin broadened and he held up a fist. The glare became a full on frown as he raised his index finger. "One. Buried treasure. Two," the middle finger came up, "booby-trapped tombs." Ring finger. "Three. Mummies and skeletons and shit. Four," he raised his pinky, "daring escapes from things trying to kill us. And five," he pulled his thumb back, revealing an open palm, "Whenever I get close to you, I hear a fucking John Williams score."

Another fat red curl popped free from her ponytail as she scowled, "Laugh it up, chuckles. I'm trying to actually *do* something to get us out of here, so you just stand there and be man-candy while the big girl figures this one out." She turned back to the writing on the wall.

"So get on with it," he shot back, reaching out with his open palm to smack her hard on the backside. "Big girl."

"Jude!" she yelled as she pitched forward, off balance. Her hand shot out to catch herself and pressed against the wall to break her stumble.

Coriander's fingers found the small outline of the scarab, and they pushed as her weight came forward. A loud groan erupted a few feet to the right and dust billowed into the chamber as the hidden door opened, allowing precious sunlight to spill down into the space.

She shrieked in excitement and ran over to the opening. "That's it! The golden steps! This is the way out, come on!" She grabbed up the satchel and lantern and pushed him to the door.

Jude dug in his heels and threw up his hands. "Wait! You don't know-"

"What color are those steps?" She pointed to the sunlight streaming on the stairs that led up and out.

"Dusty?"

"Gold, you idiot! Come on!" she shouted. Coriander stretched out her hand and reached back for him, the sunlight illuminating her frame in blinding splendor. Confidence shone like stars in her eyes. "Come on, Jude. Faith, remember?"

Faith. Was it really that simple? He was about to find out. Jude grabbed her hand and ran up the steps behind her into the light.

"I told you I would find it. I find everything," she announced with a sly grin as they emerged.

"Indiana...let it go."

The first thing Jude noticed was that the golden light he thought was sunshine was actually the illumination from a number of fiery torches staked around the perimeter of the hidden chamber. The second was that Coriander was stock still, her vision and her gun trained on a middle-aged man in a rumpled, sandy beige suit with the distinct and nauseating aroma of brimstone wafting around him. The asshole was smiling.

This was their demon. And no Ashtiru. *Fuck.*

Full dark blanketed the night sky as Alex pulled the sedan into a tiny lot near a cluster of boarded-up buildings, and threw it into park. He got out of the car, unconcerned about leaving it behind. It wouldn't matter anyway, he thought wryly. He was leaving everything behind. A rental car seemed insignificant in comparison.

He started to open the back door and grab his bag, but his hand fell before it reached the handle. Did it contain anything that would make a difference now? The scent of sand overwhelmed him on a sharp breeze. He lifted his head and sniffed into the air. The answer was no.

Alex turned and walked down the smattering of broken pavement serving as road, toward the desert.

His shoes hit soft Egyptian sand for the first time in centuries.

A bone-deep ache, swift and blinding, brought him to his knees. Alex pitched forward as a muffled cry escaped through clenched teeth, his hands shooting out to brace himself from falling over completely. As soon as his fingers threaded through sand, he groaned, the sound a mixture of pain and remembrance.

His head dipped, and snarls of dark curls fanned across his forehead, damp with sweat, even though the night was cool. Alex snuffled out a harsh breath, breathing through his nose. The tang of sand and memory filtered over his tongue with a rasp. He swallowed against the rising scream building in his lungs and raised his head to look at the sky.

The moon was full overhead, hanging so low he could have touched it if he had the strength to lift his hand. His ears searched the distance for sound, reaching out to grab onto anything that would anchor him and keep his head from spinning off his body. He blinked with furious focus as he panted for breath. He was so close, and all he needed was to keep it together long enough to finish his quest.

Alex's fingers curled into the sand for purchase as he hauled himself to his feet, the handfuls of grainy earth dripping through his fingers back onto the dunes. His eyes fell on his prize. The tomb complex wavered in the distance, backlit by the haze of moonlight.

It was sudden and primal, and had never made more sense than at this moment. He threw back his head and howled, dark and sinister, into the night. It was a warning and a battle cry all in one. His feet moved as if they were guided by an unseen hand – straight toward the tombs.

I'm coming, Ash. Daddy's coming.

CHAPTER THIRTEEN

"Where is my child?" Coriander's voice was low and tight, the words marked with venom.

The man smiled and smoothed the line of his tie. "Safe." He tilted his head to consider them both. "For now."

Jude's fingers clenched, and he realized he was standing there like the idiot Coriander had pegged him for, with his hand curled around the bag instead of a gun. He shifted on his feet, calculating the wisdom of dropping the bag and yanking out the .45s. Coriander had him covered, but the narrowing of the man's eyes told him a sudden movement would be foolish indeed.

Shadows flickered, and in the space of a blink, the man was flanked by four hissing demons. The man's eyes glittered in a sickly shade of yellow. Coriander didn't bat an eyelash, holding her arm steady.

"My daughter, asshole. Where is she?"

The suited man flicked his eyes over Coriander with arrogance, but widened as his gaze rested on the amulet around her neck. "I see you are agreeable to a trade, then." A pink tongue darted out to swipe across his bottom lip. "I'm always open to negotiation."

Jude found his voice. "No sale. Produce the girl."

"Or what?" The man's head snapped around as if it were the first time he noticed Jude was in the room.

"There is no 'or what'. You're dead either way. Save yourself the fight," Jude growled.

The man shook his head, and behind him the demons hissed, the stench of sulfur stinking up the air. "I don't think so." He turned to Coriander. "We had a deal."

Coriander's lip curled. "Choke on it."

The sound of the shot echoed in the small space before all hell broke loose.

The head of one of the demons exploded, spraying gore against the back wall, and another howled and lunged for Coriander as the other two descended on Jude. The man faded into the background, and Jude found himself on the ground, grappling, trying to evade the sharp points of teeth and claws. The bag, long fallen from his hand, had been kicked aside in the scuffle.

Coriander screamed, and the sound of more gunfire ricocheted, the smell of gunpowder mixing with fire and brimstone.

Teeth sank into his flesh, making him yell in pain, and his fists shot out to land solid blows on the two bodies pummeling at him. He managed to get his hands around one neck and twist, and the demonic bones snapped easily. Jude tossed the body off him and reached for the other.

Spittle, like acid, burned on his skin as the creature hissed and yowled on top of him. Jude kicked out with his feet, turning into a tight roll to reverse their positions. He spotted Coriander flailing over to his side, locked in her own physical confrontation. Her gun skidded across the ground, just out of his reach. It was an easier grab than getting to the bag, so he hauled back a fist and smashed it into the demon's face. Going limp, it fell back, and Jude lunged across the body, his fingers making contact with the weapon.

He popped off two slugs, taking down the thing on top of her, before swiveling up to aim for the suited man. He was gone.

"Cori? You okay?" he asked, hauling her to her feet.

"Yeah," she panted. "Got any more water?" She held up an arm, oozing with pus. At the sight, his own wounds throbbed with pain.

"Nah. We'll have to wing it. Can you go on?"

Her face set into murderous determination. "He's still got my baby. Hell, yes."

Jude grinned at her. "That's my girl."

She leaned up and pressed a hard kiss to his mouth. "Damn straight."

He trailed along the lighted corridors of the tomb complex, his nose leading the way. Alex stopped every so often and lifted his nose in the air to sniff and change direction. The smell of brimstone and sulfur was ripe in the heavy air, assaulting his sensitive nose. Underneath, a current of something familiar drifted. It was soft and light, like sunshine and smiles. He breathed deeply, sucking the scent into his lungs, letting it roll over his tongue as if tasting it would make it appear in front of him. It smelled fresh. And alive. It buried him in recognition, and all at once, his body snapped taut with awareness.

Ashtiru.

Alex's feet shot off at a dead run, his nose anchored onto the scent of his daughter. His senses latched onto it like a homing beacon, everything else falling to the side as instinct took over. He passed through rooms, climbing steps, bracing himself for a fight around every turn.

He gasped for breath as he ran, panting with every step. His hands grasped at the walls, fingers digging in and breaking off chunks of ancient stone as he hauled himself around corners. Growling brought him up short, skidding him to a stop as two demons appeared out of nowhere, hissing and snarling. Evil yellow eyes glowed back at him, and saliva pooled and dripped from their gaping mouths. Mottled flesh pulled back over razor-sharp teeth, and they lunged.

Clawed, gnarled fingers reached for him and he stepped back, but he was too close. The pointed nails scratched at his flesh, ripping and tearing into his shirt, dragging him forward. Brimstone burned his eyes, making them water. He yelled and flailed, knocking one to the side, giving him enough room to try to spin out of the clutching grasp.

It didn't work, and it advanced, pulling him closer. Saliva ran from the open maw, dropping onto his neck. His skin burned, and his hands shot up to close around the neck. He gripped hard and squeezed, listening for the tell-tale snap of bones. The thing wheezed, and he adjusted his hands, grabbing the face. He twisted hard and snapped the demon's neck with a sickening crack. It fell back, limp, onto the ground, but there was no time to regroup before the second one launched its attack.

They fell to the ground in a tangle of limbs, both of them snarling and lashing out with frenzied abandon. Alex writhed and shifted his body, trying to avoid the onslaught of claws and teeth. He slammed his knee up into the demon's torso, knocking the wind out of it, and threw it off. His fingers scrabbled for purchase on the floor, and he regained his footing. The demon howled and snaked its hand around his ankle, pulling hard to drag him back down. Alex's foot shot out and caught it in the face, and it rolled over on its back with a gurgle.

The demon's chest heaved with labored breaths and Alex threw himself down, straddling its chest. His head reared back, and with a bellow that originated from his toes, stabbed his hands into the diseased flesh. Alex's fingers curled as the skin gave way, and he yanked his hands apart, tearing open the chest cavity. The demon screamed, and he tore harder, until the sound faded into a bubbling whine before it went silent.

Alex snorted and jumped up, shaking the gore from his hands. He burned from head to toe, covered in the poisonous fluids. Ashtiru's scent came back to him in a flood, and he closed his eyes, concentrating. Ignoring the pain, he ran on, tracking the smell.

Alex raced, his heart pounding in his chest, lungs burning with each labored inhale and exhale. Deep inside, the jackal roused, growling to life with purpose. It flooded his nerves, saturating his brain with consciousness and fighting against his humanity. He passed by another open room when a soft whimper stopped him in his tracks. He backpedaled and ran inside.

The chamber was large and empty, with one small torch burning inside the door to cast a dim, flickering light within. The scent was strongest here, and his nose twitched in triumph. The rumble from his chest startled him as his eyes focused inside. Something small was huddled against the wall, almost near the corner, shaking with soft tremors. The hiss of breath that escaped him echoed, causing it to move. Alex locked eyes with his daughter and sank to his knees in the doorway. The rush overwhelmed him, and blue light shot from around him as the jackal in him howled with relief.

He crawled forward on hands and knees, and scooped up the child into his arms, the pulse of light growing stronger as it trailed around the chamber and out into the corridors.

"I'm here, Princess. Daddy's here."

As he gathered her closer, the jackal surfaced, unwilling to be denied any longer. Alex threw back his head and howled out loud, the deep sound trilling in the air like a benediction.

Jude and Coriander ran back out into the hallway, searching for any sign of the suited man. Her reclaimed weapon hung loosely in her hand.

"Come on," she shouted, taking his hand. "This way."

He followed hot on her heels, tamping down the urge to rush ahead of her. The feeling tasted strange in his mouth, but he swallowed it down with instinct to trust that she knew what she was doing.

A shadow rippled past, and Coriander's arm lifted to pop off two rounds as they entered another room. The light chuckle brought them up short and face to face with their quarry.

The man smiled with ease, but his face paled as a sliver of blue light drifted in, covering them all.

The ripple of blue light pulsed through the chamber, resonating off the walls with an eerie howl. The hairs on the back of Jude's neck stood on end, and Coriander's eyes grew wide with recognition. Her lips turned upward in a menacing sneer.

"You can't hide her now," Coriander said. "You can't keep her from me." Her voice grew in cadence, gaining strength as she spoke. "He'll find her. He'll sniff her out." She shook her head, escaped strands of auburn hair flying through the air as she laughed. "If you thought you had your hands full with me, just you wait." Her eyes glittered as she tracked the haze of blue mist that still lingered. Another howl vibrated through the walls. "Call more of them if you want. It doesn't matter now. He'll take them all." Her smile was pure malice. "The Anubis has come home."

"He has no home," the man snapped back. "His death is mine as surely as yours is. We had a deal, and The Dealer has come to collect his prize." He snarled as his yellow eyes flashed with hate, and two demons appeared behind Jude, taking him to the ground from behind.

Coriander yelled and fired again, missing The Dealer by a fraction.

"Give me what I want, you bitch!" he screamed, lunging and grabbing for her.

Jude grappled, twisting to get free, but claws and teeth held him tight, and he was helpless to get a handhold on anything. He could only watch as The Dealer knocked the gun from Coriander's grasp and pulled her to him.

"Get him up," he told the demons, and Jude was hauled without ceremony to his feet and shoved against a crumbling sarcophagus, forgotten in a corner of the room.

Alex stared into his daughter's face, dirty and streaked with tears. She held his hands gently and laced her tiny fingers in his. Green eyes that reminded him of the hills of Greece gazed back at him, as if they held all the wonder in the world in their depths. Ashtiru's face softened and she spoke, but the voice that emanated from her was not her own.

"Destiny calls, and weeps at the feet of children. It rides on the wings of angels, soaring ever higher until at last it knows its purpose. It rises like the tide and sweeps away the regrets of yesteryear and all the iniquity of days long past. Embrace it, and know these next moments are what you were born for." She shuddered as bright tears filled her eyes.

"Daddy?" The innocence crept back into her true voice. "It's okay, Daddy. He has you now. He has us all." She smiled, full of life and promise. "I love you," she whispered.

He gathered her in his arms, and felt her little body shudder and go slack. Alex smoothed her hair back over her face as he laid her down softly against the wall. He pressed a small kiss to the shell of her ear. "I love you too, Princess," he whispered before rising to his feet. The beginnings of power long buried simmered in his veins as it made the long trek to the surface.

He turned into the darkness, steeling himself to rail against the forces of Hell. Alex smiled, the feral curl of his lips splitting the dry skin. He tasted blood and the rage of the Father. He was pleased.

Growls filled the chamber as bodies piled in. Alex stared down the pack of demons, standing in front of Ashtiru, shielding the child with his body. The demons groaned and moved forward, evil yellow fire flashing from their eyes. He knew there were dozens more, so many more, positioned elsewhere in the tomb complex. Possibly spilling out into the desert, ready to make their way to find more living souls to turn. But he would not let them take her. He drew himself up, feeling the power coursing through him like the cool flow of Nile waters. He gave into it, spreading his arms wide. He was ready.

Light and sensation buzzed in his head, making everything hazy and clear all at once. It was time.

A voice filtered in over the white noise in his brain, instantly soothing his nerves. "You have served Me well. Fulfill this destiny, and rest, knowing you have stars in your crown and acres in Heaven."

The blue light over his swirled and brightened, illuminating every dark corner, and he snarled in delight as the demons shielded their eyes. The jackal within him stirred, growling to life as the light drifted outward, gaining in brilliance. Power curled up from his toes, igniting every nerve in his body, filling him with radiance. The walls shook and the ground rumbled as Alex called the light within him. His hands shot out, palms lifted heavenward, as lightning coiled in their centers.

Alex's head dipped as he closed his eyes and murmured, "I am ready, Father. I will live as I have served. For eternity."

The lightning in his hand shot upward and Alex's head jerked back, his mouth open and gaping as the blue light burst and channeled inside. His body glowed from the inside out as stones fell from the walls and the ground lurched beneath his feet. He felt it burn and claw in his belly, reaching a fevered pitch until he couldn't contain it any longer. His body spasmed, and he screamed into the chamber, releasing the divine light in a shout of exaltation.

The walls burst into a shower of dust, the high-pitched wail of Alex's cry careening around the space in an echo of vengeance. The demons fell, one by one, their bodies exploding in a series of sickening pops. He pushed the light out, far beyond the one chamber, letting it seek and destroy in its wake, decimating stone and darkness. He felt Ashtiru behind him, huddled and frightened, but there was nothing more he could do for her but this. One day she would understand, but for now all he could process was destruction. The blue light snaked from his eyes, carving its way through the chambers, and with each demon that fell, Alex felt himself grow stronger.

The jackal's face filled his vision, delirious with want, and his heart soared. This was his gift, the greatest protection he could provide, wrapped within the dark tide of destruction. The blue light curled again, this time to cocoon Ashtiru in its rays, the child crumpled in a soft heap on the ground, dust and debris bouncing off of her like raindrops.

Joyous voices filtered in over his brain, calling him, beseeching him for one last act. He followed their song and shouted in triumph as he flung out the last of the light within him.

"My God!" he cried into the light, "I am done!"

A bright blue flash of light exploded around him before the chamber shuddered and went dark.

Thunder crashed, shaking the tomb, threatening to send everyone to their knees as a keening howl sounded over the tumble of stone. Coriander cried out as The Dealer tightened his hold and regained his balance.

Behind him the wall shuddered, and an opening appeared within the stone, the choking stench of sulfur and brimstone leeching into the chamber. The void was black and swirling, growing wider by precious inches. The sound of screaming and maniacal laughter drifted in, deafening the thunder that shook the tomb.

"You see, angel? You cannot win. The dark will not be denied," he grinned. "My Lord will have what He wants and there is nothing you can do stop him!" The

Dealer's smile widened as he cackled in glee. "He will have them all and you will kneel at His splendor!"

Jude's eyes caught Coriander's and her leg twitched in response. Before he could tell her to stop, she raised her foot and brought it down on The Dealer's at the same time her sharp little elbow slammed into the older man's gut. He grunted in pain and staggered enough to ease his hold. She whirled, shoving a fist into his face with a snap of bone on bone. She screamed as he gripped the pendant and wrenched it from her neck.

"Now!" she cried, jumping back from his reach, but not before The Dealer's fist came up to backhand Coriander to the ground. She cried out and crumpled, pressing a hand to her bleeding face.

Rage filled him as Jude leaped to the side, his hands finding purchase on the lid of the sarcophagus, pushing it off with all his might. More dust filled the chamber, and he saw Coriander duck and roll as The Dealer popped off two shots in her direction. There, on top of the mummy, gleaming brightly, was a staff. Jude wrapped his hands around it and held it aloft.

The earth gave a loud groan and The Dealer's eyes went wide with fear as the staff in Jude's hand transformed into a sword, the blade burning with golden fire. A host of angelic voices echoed through the space, the song cresting higher as Jude shook his hand into the air. All at once, he was filled with light and purpose, and it vibrated in his bones with delicious agony.

"Father!" Jude called. "I am here!"

Golden sparks shot out from the end of the blade and Jude doubled over in pain. His body jerked back on a cry of salvation as the tattoo on his back rippled and flared to life, golden wings erupting in a wave of brilliance. They fanned out in a shower of feathers as the heavenly hosts cheered in triumph.

Jude straightened and swung the sword, the blade arcing through the dark. A burst of light filled the room as a thunderous voice shouted into the air.

"Fear Me and the glory of My wrath! Vengeance has returned!"

All the rage and anger in his soul melted as faith sang in his blood, filling him with righteousness. The sword swung again, followed by Jude's blood-curdling howl. The Dealer screamed, but was cut silent as the flaming blade removed his head from his body.

Blood and black gore spouted from the stump as the body twitched where it stood. The sound of screaming and terror shot up out of the body, and tendrils of black smoke spewed into the air. As the corpse fell, Coriander scrabbled to reach for the pendant, still clenched in The Dealer's hand.

"No! Don't touch it!" Jude cried.

The portal behind The Dealer's remains rippled and grew, advancing on them. Jude pulled her back before her fingers could grab the necklace. The earth trembled as the chasm widened, and a rush of fire shot out from its depths to encompass the body. It burned hot and high, stinking of death and despair as it formed a barrier over the corpse, and he and Coriander could only watch as the fiery pool was sucked into the void.

When the thick, black smoke dissipated, nothing remained but the sound of thunder and the tremble of stone. The pendant was gone.

CHAPTER FOURTEEN

Jude helped Coriander to her feet, pulling her close to wrap his arms around her. He snorted over the top of her head as he surveyed the scorched stone.

"I fucking hate Egypt," he huffed into her hair.

She chuckled against him. "It may be a while before I can bring myself to come back." Coriander's head lifted with a smile. "Come on, let's go find Alex and Ash."

He stared down with sober eyes. "Are you sure they're still alive?"

She placed a hand over her heart and nodded. "Yeah. Call it mother's intuition."

They raced down the corridors, Coriander calling out for Ashtiru at the top of her lungs. The walls were charred with soot, and stone crumbled and crashed as they ran.

"We need to hurry," Jude said. "Whatever rocked this place was serious. I don't know if it's going to stand for much longer."

She shot him a smirk over her shoulder. "Please. This place has survived for thousands of years. I don't think one showdown with Hell is going to put a chink in its armor."

The high-pitched whine of a dog caught his ears, and he pulled her to a stop in front of a ravaged doorway. Coriander ducked inside without a word, dragging him along.

"Ashtiru!" she cried.

Sure enough, sitting against the wall, covered in soot and dust, was Ashtiru, clinging tightly to a buff-colored dog. Jude's breath left him in a rush as Coriander whispered, "Alex."

Jude stared at the dog, which was panting happily with a long pink tongue lolling out of its mouth, as Coriander rushed forward to take the little girl into her arms. The dog got up and circled them, nosing Coriander in the elbow. She laid an affectionate hand on the animal's head.

"Oh, you," she said through tears. "You precious, precious man."

The dog eased out from under her touch to step back and bark once, its tail wagging with enthusiasm.

Coriander stood, hefting the girl onto her hip. Ashtiru raised a sleepy head and yawned.

"Can we go home now, Mommy?"

She pressed a soft kiss onto her daughter's cheek and looked straight at Jude. "Of course, darling."

Ashtiru lowered her head back onto her mother's shoulder with a sigh. "Daddy Jude, too?"

Emotion clenched his heart at the soft-spoken question. He stood there for a moment, hanging at the edge of his future, his body pained and tired. His wings hung like weights on his back, yet he had never felt lighter. What he did now would set his path for the rest of his life. Heaven had been restored to him, but the pull of Earth rested in the innocent wonder of a child and the tear-shiny emerald eyes of the woman he loved. The conviction of steel-sharp faith tingled over him, resonating with only one option.

Jude stepped forward and embraced them both, leaning down to whisper into their ears, "Daddy Jude, too."

Coriander turned her face upward, wet with tears. He kissed her on the forehead and squeezed them tighter.

She stepped free of his hold and headed to the door, calling over her shoulder, "Let's go, you two. I've got to call in a few favors to get us on the next flight out without Customs."

"You think we'll have issues?"

She swung around and pursed her lips. "Sword. Dog. Do the math."

Jude glanced down at his hand. The golden sword gleamed, the surface pristine and glowing. "You may have a point. Really though, what about him?" He gestured to the dog.

"I won't leave him behind."

He nodded at the firmness in her tone. "I wouldn't ask you to."

The animal whined, thumping its tail on the floor before coming over to sniff at Jude's thigh.

He glowered down. "Yeah, remember that. And if you even think of hiking your leg near me, I'll neuter you myself with a coat hanger and a rusty spoon."

The dog's tongue dripped and shook as it panted, and Jude swore he could see a spark of the old Alex in there somewhere. His hypothesis was confirmed when the animal lifted his leg and pissed down Jude's leg.

"Coriander!"

The happy reunion was quickly cut short by Coriander shushing everyone in the living room, putting her hand over Ashtiru's sleeping head. She passed the child off to her mother, and Khemrhy whisked her away upstairs, sparing a heartfelt glance at Coriander and then at Jude. He smiled back at the goddess.

Lucius was the first to grab him and pull him into a giant hug. He flinched out of habit, but relaxed as he realized there was no pain.

"I still don't think I'm a hug it out kind of guy," he smirked.

Lucius set him back with a look of surprise. "What?"

Jude chuckled. "It doesn't hurt, but I don't swing that way."

"The pain? It's gone?" Elijah signed.

He nodded. "Gone."

"And your wings?" Mordecai asked, his face tight.

Jude chucked off his shirt, and ignored the good-natured catcalling from Coriander, Persephone, and Teraslynn. All voices fell silent when he turned and fluffed out the golden wings. He flexed them once for good measure before turning back around. He frowned as he noticed the absence of one body.

"Where's Dom?"

"Pool house. Don't push it. I'll tell him you're back."

"He knows," a voice said from the back of the living room.

Jude's head swiveled to see Domniel standing just inside the house, half-in and half-out onto the back patio. No one heard him open the French doors.

"You make it back in one piece?" Domniel asked. His voice was rough around the edges, and he looked like he hadn't slept in days.

"Yeah," Jude said, voice catching in his throat. "With new accessories." He gave the wings a gentle flap.

"I know. I could smell them when I opened the doors." He lifted his nose into the air and sniffed. "I smell dog, too. And not Lige. His scent is changing."

"Alex, er, the Anubis, came back, and he's sort of...different," Jude explained.

Domniel made no move to come inside the house any further, and Jude couldn't bring himself to make his way across the floor. "I think that's probably an understatement."

"Maybe," Jude laughed.

"Jude?"

"Yeah, brother?"

"Good job." With that, he backed out and shut the doors.

Alex trotted over and barked out at the glass.

Mordecai gave Jude a grin, and said, "So...Alex, huh? That's got to be interesting."

"I guess we'll see," he answered.

"I'm sensing there will be a little awkwardness when Cori asks you to walk her ex," Mordecai chuckled.

"Shut up, Cai."

Elijah nudged at his deaf brother, but he continued, "Think he'll sleep at the foot of the bed? That's a little kinky, even for me."

This time, Lucius and Jude spoke in unison, "Shut up, Cai!"

Mordecai's snicker was cut off by Khemrhy's voice drifting down from the stairs. "Jude, I thank you for returning my loved ones to me." Her gaze fell on her daughter. "Coriander, can I see you in your office, please?"

She nodded and passed by him, pressing a kiss to his cheek. "I'll see you upstairs, yeah?"

"In a little while. There's somebody I have to talk to."

Coriander turned from the bookshelves as Khemhry walked in and shut the door behind them.

"Mother."

"Daughter."

"You didn't stop him."

"No. I did not."

Coriander pitched forward and braced her hands on the back of her desk chair. "Why?" Coriander cried out, the sound of her heart breaking evident in the shrill despair of her voice. "How could you? How could you let him go, knowing what would happen? Why didn't you try to stop him?"

Khemrhy advanced on her, the folds of her sari whipping around her ankles in a fierce jangle. "Because," she snapped. "Because it was not my place to hold him back. Because I do not defy that which I believe. Sometimes death is an ending, and sometimes it is a beginning. It is not up to me to decide which. You should know by now that time is not measured by death. It was his time, Coriander. And you should remember that he embraced it for you."

Coriander glared back at her. "All this time I thought you were so powerful, even if I didn't know what it meant. Was I wrong, Mother?"

"Stupid child," the goddess hissed. "How dare you question the authority of my will? My will is His will, as it has always been. Didn't I teach you that? Haven't I always given you the truth, even when you didn't want it?" Coriander's lips trembled and the mother in her wanted to bite her tongue, but the goddess inside raged at the hubris. "You bark at me like the animal Alex has become, when instead you should be falling to your knees and thanking Him for the blessings which brought you home! Mourn Alex's loss because you loved him, not because you think I betrayed you by not saving him." Khemhry drew herself up and folded her hands. "I've kissed my granddaughter good night and I have lauded your lover for bringing you back to me. Perhaps when you've got your head on straight, you'll come to me and we can have this conversation again. Until then, I'm going home."

The goddess paraded out the front door in a jangle of clinking bracelets and the rustle of silk, her divine presence trailing behind. As she walked down the steps to the driveway, the mother held her face in her hands and sobbed.

Sunrise threatened to break over the horizon, the first rays of sunshine taking the chill off the dawn. Jude stretched his legs out in front of him, his feet scraping on the shingles of the roof. He closed his eyes and turned his face heavenward, fanning his wings out behind him with a satisfied sigh.

"I am proud of you, Jude." The Voice spoke with affection.

"I'm a little proud of me, too."

"You've come far."

"I'm ready to keep going."

He opened his eyes to see the sky swirl in a haze of orange and purple. Everything seemed fresh, brighter, and full of purpose. Jude's heart sank with a guilty twinge.

"Don't worry. He looks upon the same sunrise. Only with different eyes."

Alex.

Jude shook his head. "I know, but I still feel like we left a man behind." His hands curled into fists at his side. "We don't work that way. We don't leave anyone behind. He may not have been one of us in truth, but in a way, he was. And I know she's upset about that."

"She will grieve. It is the nature of love." The Voice said with sympathy.

"I would spare her that pain if I could."

"All you can do is love her. Love them all."

"And what about him? Is he really Alex? Inside?"

A breeze drifted over him, slipping over his skin with comfort.

"In a sense," The Voice said. "His humanity is gone, but his loyalty and devotion to his daughter are unshakeable. He still has a destiny ahead of him. Do not worry about his future. I hold him in My hands."

"Does Ash understand that her father is gone? I don't want her to grow up and hate me for trying to take his place. I don't want her to forget him."

"Then keep his memory alive. Love her as he would. She will understand, and one day she will praise you for it. But he will be with her in other ways."

"The dog?"

"Yes," The Voice answered. "He will befriend her, guide her, and protect her. The Anubis has power of his own. He will only draw his last breath when she does. Take comfort in knowing he will be with her when you cannot."

"There's something coming, isn't there? We lost her necklace, and I don't know what that means, but I can guess it's not good. We're not safe," Jude said, feeling the tingle of dread at the back of his skull.

The sky darkened for an instant, then returned to its blaze of color.

"Guard your sword arm, Vengeance. My enemy seeks to usurp me, and I will need all My warriors to drive him back."

"I am ever Your servant," Jude said, bowing his head.

"You lived in pain for so long, My child. You denied yourself the gift of faith. Not in Me, but in yourself. Do not lose that. It will sustain you when the path is unclear."

"Father." The word slipped out on a choked cry.

"Faith, Jude. It is as endless as My love. Have faith."

The presence of The Voice faded into the distance as daybreak burst across the horizon. Jude pressed a hand over his heart and thought of laughing green eyes and the tinkle of a little girl's laughter.

Faith.

Lucifer doubled over with a sharp stab of pain that nearly drove him to his knees. He held his bloody hands in front of his face, flexing them against the wet stickiness that remained. He knew what the pain meant with picture-perfect clarity. The Dealer had failed.

Damn.

He eased to a stand, his eyes flicking over the mangled bodies before him. The women were nothing more than a gruesome pile of limbs and flesh. Neither had given him the answer he wanted. The whereabouts of the Incubus were still unknown. Killing them had served no purpose whatsoever, not even to soothe his rage. It left him empty. Unfulfilled.

He had let them beg, hoping beyond hope that their tearful cries would do something to smooth over his anger at being denied his quarry. The meek one had to go first; he could smell the demon seed on her as soon as he barreled into the tent. There was no way he could leave her alive to deliver whatever hellspawn she had growing in her womb. It was faint, she wasn't far along, but he could take no chances in allowing the thing to grow. So he had ripped her apart with his bare hands.

The other one put up more of a fight, daring to come at him with an offensive assault, then struck back when he manhandled her to the ground. She had been harder to subdue, but in the end, her fragile mortality shredded under his hands like the other. Her final gasp of "Khemrhy" enraged him further, and his hands curled into her throat with a ferocity that had his fingers digging into muscle and sinew until they met, tangled in the inner workings of her neck.

And he was still empty, panting with exertion, his body shaking in fine tremors that radiated out from his chest and down his limbs to his fingers and toes. He was empty. The Dealer had failed, and he was no closer to the Incubus.

It wasn't supposed to be like this. There was supposed to be glory and rewards beyond measure, and while there had been brief moments of something that could have passed for that, there had been precious little of either. He realized now that the freedom he coveted, even though it came with a longer leash than service, was tied at the inevitable end with a noose that squeezed just as tight.

And you're about to swing, aren't you, old boy?

Lucifer gritted his teeth and backed out of the tent, instinct guiding his steps to the babbling pool in the heart of the old temple. He jumped in with both feet and scrubbed himself clean, before crawling out and shaking himself off like a dog. He closed his eyes and blew out a harsh, clearing breath. There was no choice now. No free will. He had to run. He had to hide. He had to find the

Incubus if he had any hope of showing his face in Hell again. And he had to do it before his Lord found him.

Fear welled in the back of his throat, thick and bitter. It wasn't supposed to be like this.

He took off like a shot into the dark night, as if his life depended on it. Because it did.

EPILOGUE

Blood dripped in a slick trail from the battered curl of his giant fists as he shuffled forward, the crimson drops hissing as they made contact with the heated floor of the chamber. The wall of fire in front of him flared into life, burning and crackling with bright orange flames. In seconds, sweat poured off of him, trailing down his naked skin to mix with the blood on his body and form a smoking pink pool at his gnarled, dirty feet. He stared into the fire with a hateful glare as the flames shifted and parted, allowing a dark-suited man to step forward.

"I come to you in the flesh, Artesal, and still you will not kneel?" Amusement lurked behind the steel bite of the question.

"No." The word was rasped out over dry lips, in a voice husky with disuse.

The suited man smiled, his black eyes twinkling in the firelight as he shoved his hands into his trouser pockets. The dark fringe of his hair spilled over his forehead as he laughed. "Oh, My beast, how beautifully you deny Me." He stepped forward in front of Artesal, unruffled in the intense heat of the room. "And yet you serve."

"I serve but one master," Artesal replied, meeting the black gaze.

The man's smile grew larger. "As it pleases Me." A hand reached up to brush across Artesal's cheek. The touch was fleeting, sending a light shiver over his skin. The man's head tilted to the side. "Well?"

Artesal lowered his gaze to his bloody fists. "It is done."

The man gave a sharp intake of breath as he rocked back on his heels. "Good. I hope you made My displeasure known. The Dealer failed as sure as his predecessor. Punishment was inevitable." His gaze flicked over the blood on Artesal's naked form. "I see you have delivered."

"As it pleases You."

A low chuckle slipped from the man's lips as he dragged a thumbnail across Artesal's chest, scraping through the blood and sweat. "It does."

Artesal raised his eyes, sighing with tired resignation. "Am I finished?"

A twinge of annoyance crossed the man's features at Artesal's question, pinching the lines of his face and causing his brow to furrow. It came and went, and soon the man's face was smooth and relaxed again. He stared into Artesal's eyes, the black pools widening with intense scrutiny before he rose on tiptoe to press cool, dry lips against Artesal's forehead. The kiss tingled as a sickening dread spread out over Artesal's skin.

"No," the man replied. "I have one more task for you." He caught the faint scent of flowers, sunshine, and spring on the man's breath as he moved his face to whisper in Artesal's ear, "Bring Me the Morning Star."

Artesal blinked, offering no other response as he turned to leave.

He breached the threshold of the chamber when Satan's voice called out to him, "Oh, and Artesal?"

Artesal stopped, but didn't bother to turn and give the devil his due.

"Hurt him just a little bit."

COMING 2015 - THE NEXT
CHAPTER OF THE FALLEN

ELIJAH
THE FALLEN

MORE ABOUT THE AUTHORS

Tara S. Wood

Tara Wood divides her time between creating domestic bliss and creating hot paranormal romance with the occasional side of kink. When not playing June Cleaver for her hubby and daughter, she can be found at the local Starbucks slamming back Frappuccinos and plotting out her next idea. Or she's watching the BBC. Tara resides with her wonderful and tolerant family in the suburbs of Houston, Texas. She is currently at work on several projects, one of them being the next book in her In Blood series.

Lorecia Goings

Lorecia is a native Houstonian who did not escape in her adulthood. So she camps out in NW Houston concocting her own special variety of chaos but rarely finishes it without the continual prodding of best friend Tara. She loves to laugh, bead, write, eat and hug kitties. She also loves to have fun and can usually be found on any given Friday night off chatting her head off at Denny's with her bestie.

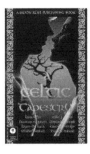  

Bringing the impossible to life through our pages.

16434497R00123

Printed in Poland
by Amazon Fulfillment
Poland Sp. z o.o., Wrocław